T0079704

Karolinum Press

Ladislav Grosman (1921–1981) was born in Humenné, Slovakia to a Jewish family. The son of a tanner father and a shopkeeper mother, Grosman was a talented student but was prevented from graduating secondary school due to anti-Jewish legislation when Slovakia became a puppet state of Nazi Germany in 1939. He worked as a laborer in a brick factory before being conscripted into (unarmed) military service. After an unsuccessful escape attempt, he was sent to a forced labor camp. He went into hiding after the Slovak National Uprising of 1944, the same year his parents and three of his siblings died during the German attack on Ružomberok. After the end of the war, he returned briefly to Humenné in order to obtain his diploma.

He soon moved to Prague to study, earning an advanced degree from the University of Political and Social Sciences. He then went on to work in publishing, while at the same time studying educational psychology. During this time he also began to write seriously – first in Slovak and then in Czech. His novella, *The Shop on Main Street*, was adapted into a film that became the first Czechoslovak movie to win an Academy Award. Ján Kádar, who co-wrote the screenplay with Grosman and directed the movie with Elmar Klos, said the short novel "appealed to Klos and myself by its special angle of truthfulness, the tragicomedy of the story and the author's humanistic approach." In 1965 Grosman became a screenwriter for the acclaimed Barrandov Studios; in 1967 he received his doctorate in psychology.

Grosman emigrated to Israel the month following 1968's Soviet-led invasion and occupation of Czechoslovakia. He spent the rest of his life teaching Slavic literature and creative writing at Bar-Ilan University.

MODERN CZECH CLASSICS

Ladislav Grosman
The Shop
on Main Street

Translated from the Czech by Iris Urwin Lewitová
Afterword by Benjamin Frommer

KAROLINUM PRESS 2019

KAROLINUM PRESS
Karolinum Press is a publishing department
of Charles University
Ovocný trh 5/560, 116 36 Prague 1
Czech Republic
www.karolinum.cz

Cover illustration by Jiří Grus
Designed by Zdeněk Ziegler
Copyedited by Mark Corner
Set and printed in the Czech Republic by Karolinum Press
Second English edition, first by Karolinum

Cataloging-in-Publication Data is available from the National Library
of the Czech Republic

ISBN 978-80-246-4022-8 (pb)
ISBN 978-80-246-4021-1 (ebk)

ONE

The clouds dispersed as the anger of the sudden storm departed and the wind made the most of the respite, blowing and veering, buffeting them into odd shapes and chasing them all over the sky. Blue patches appeared above, lit up by the sun and by the reflection of fiery blows rising from the earth below.

Hammers were ringing on the anvil, clear and solemn like weighty bells of precious bronze. The clanging gave a new burst of energy to a flying stork. With joyful flapping of wings, it found a favorable current and took a short cut home to the nest. Swooping over the church steeple, over scattered shingle roofs and tin roofs, it rose in the air for one more view of the little town among the hills and then glided down in a steep dive, straight for the nest, encouraged by the children calling from the road: "Storks are homing, babies coming!" The great black and white bird lowered its legs, gave a last flap of its wings, and settled on the straggly nest near the smithy.

This left the children free to watch the bearded smith in his big leather apron and to admire his bold sleight of hand as he seized a horse's leg. The inexperienced foal jerked its head and reared, struggling to escape the relentless grip. The mare harnessed to a farm cart a few feet away neighed angrily, but the foal resisted the fire and the paring knife.

Wisps of blue smoke twisted up from the scorched hoof. "Scram!" The smith turned on the children. "Get out of here and find someplace else to play." As if they were in his way! Still, it was never wise to be around when Balko the smith got worked up, and so the kids went off.

Hell-fire and brimstone,
Let the smith pass;
The pony's broken loose
And kicked him in the ass!

They chanted in chorus; he wasn't going to get away with it. One voice started and the rest took it up, even the tiniest. There were seven of them at play, barefoot little urchins darting to and fro, grandchildren of the drummer from the yard, the tobacconist's kids, and some from the neighboring cottages. A girl, pigtail flapping and her skirt above her knees, was hopping along with a jump rope.

The children started chasing each other, jumping up and down and squealing as they swerved round the linden trees on the edge of the sidewalk. The smallest of the lot, a freckled boy of six or so with short, bristly hair, tried to get possession of the jump rope by tickling the back of the girl's neck, just under the plait of hair. She hung on to her precious toy, and they started a tug of war, back and forth, pulling and tugging, the others taking sides and shouting encouragement, until all at once the boy jerked backward and fell on his backside. Laughter and wails mingled, and the children disappeared like thieves behind the yard gate.

The little girl was left on the street, skipping first on one foot and then on the other and then both together. She stood still for a minute, pitying a little donkey drawing a huge barrel of stable manure. The poor little thing could hardly put one foot before the other; it was no use the driver's yelling "Gee up! Gee up!" as though testing his voice in order to keep his own spirits up. It was hot, and the sun beat mercilessly down.

The sound of the boys shouting in the yard brought the girl in after them. With a hop, a skip, and a jump she went over to the ladder and the makeshift dog kennel, hens and chickens clucking and flapping round her feet, and didn't stop until she had reached the line of snowy wash hanging between two old walnut trees.

The carpenter appeared in the shadow of the half-open door on the other side of the yard. The children could not be sure Brtko's wife would not appear, too, heftier and more to be feared. Brtko scratched behind one ear, wondering, probably, whether to bother to hear his wife out to the end.

"It won't cost you anything and they can't bite your head off." Her voice came from within the kitchen.

"We'll see," he answered. "It's no good forcing things, Eveline, and I'm not going on my knees to them, neither."

He stepped out.

The dog squeezed out between his master's felt boots and shot over to the children on the grass. He was a mongrel, white with a yellow smudge over his right eye.

As the door slammed, the little girl's voice rose in greeting: "Praise be to the Lord!"

Brtko the carpenter turned to face the children, one hand making sure his folding rule was in its right place in his back pocket. The children said nothing. The carpenter straightened his baize apron over his chest and scratched his short hair thoughtfully. "For ever and ever, amen," he mumbled in the direction of the little girl crouching on the grass with the rest, watching the scene as though it were a play.

"Nugget!" Brtko called the dog to him, and they went out of the yard together. A train whistled not far off.

The smith at his open forge was too busy to break off and chat with him, even if Brtko had had it in mind to stop; but he was in a hurry, too. As he passed the low cottage windows, he peered into some and found the dark dwellings uncared-for and deserted.

There was something up, although nobody else in the street seemed to notice it. Even the dog looked up at his master, puzzled. Brtko checked on the time, in case he had made a mistake, and shook his head uncomprehendingly. All the years he had lived near the station he had never known them to close the level crossing at this hour of the day.

It was a train–a special train, not in the timetable, and it roared past as though the engine driver were afraid he'd be in for it if he didn't reach the end of the world before sunset.

Brtko and the dog stepped back a few paces. Dust and noise came swirling out from under the wheels, and the military train blocked their view of the main street beyond the line. Nugget gave vent to his dissatisfaction in short barks, but in the dreadful uproar Brtko could not hear him; he could only see the angry jerking, and it irritated him all the more. Trucks loaded with guns and manned by soldiers in camouflage uniforms flashed by as the train clattered past at speed.

At last the brake van at the end of the train roared away out of sight, and they both felt relieved. The sun came out from behind the clouds.

The one-armed tobacconist was sitting beneath his enamel TOBACCONIST AND OFFICIAL STAMPS sign, staring out at the sleepy street. It was all he could do to keep awake in the afternoons; as soon as the days grew warm, he would drag his shabby old cane chair out and sit in the sun. He came to slowly, not realizing at first that the dog was by him. "Naughty dog," he said with a little smile.

"Hi there, Gejza," the carpenter called out.

"Woke me up, he did–the devil take him. You're not getting anything out of me today, mate."

The man was pleased at how the dog pricked up his ears, looking from one to the other as if he knew it was all put on for his benefit.

"Not even a pinch of backy for a pipe?"

"Not a single pinch."

"Not even enough to roll a ciggie?"

"No."

"Oh, come on, just a pinch."

"No."

"Not even a fag end?"

"No, no, no!"

Then the scene reached its climax: as the tobacconist repeated his determined refusal, Nugget gave three short, sharp barks, and the two friends laughed, seeing that their joke had worked yet again.

Nugget had played his role, sitting up and begging in order to soften the tobacconist's heart. Brtko took three cigarettes from the case generously held out towards him and slipped them into his breast pocket.

Between the butcher's shop and the municipal weighbridge the dogs were waiting for their share of the bones. The horse-drawn cart had come out of the slaughterhouse yard, and it was high time. Today there was a bigger pack than usual-rumors of a generous hand must have been spread from kennel to kennel all over the town. Sensing the greater risk of competition, the dogs were getting irritable and worrying the mare.

Growling angrily and impatiently, the dogs demanded their customary rights.

The butcher's assistant stood in the doorway in his white apron, a bucket under his arm, and waited for the right moment to throw the next lot of bones into the middle of the pack.

Brtko was uneasy and took good care to keep an eye on Nugget, the only dog not rushing at the prize. He stood there waiting for the word, hard though it was for him. "Go!" Brtko gave the order at a moment when the dogs were all busy with another lot of bones and failed to notice one that had fallen to one side. Nugget leaped through the air and landed right on his target.

"Good times ahead, it seems," said his master, dreamily watching the busier end of the street, near the square.

Brtko turned impatiently as the sound of a trumpet rang out. The trumpeter—as yet unseen though no one could miss the sound of him-seemed to be intent on drowning out the noise of the street with his blaring instrument. Obviously this was no ordinary occasion. The dragoons had only been quartered in the town a few days before.

The people on the sidewalks stood still, and the windows were in full bloom with women's heads fair and dark and smiling girls' faces. The trumpet sounded even louder, and round the corner came the village priest riding a bicycle. Behind him, as though the figure in a cassock had a secret mission to show the soldiers which way to follow, rode an officer, erect in the saddle. Then down the narrow trough of the street flowed the stream of hussars, two by two, in time to the march, as though the most important thing in the world was the impression they were making on the onlookers and the remarks being passed on the elegance of their trotting.

With smiling faces, the dragoons returned the greetings waved from the windows and sidewalks, but the trumpeter blew into the sounding brass with cheeks puffed out, no thought for the approving nods and cries of the onlookers, no eye for Brtko and his dog, not even for the barefoot imps of mischief.

Into the thud of hooves, the sound of the church bells fell softly. There were three grey pigeons on the steeple roof, and the hands of the black clock in the shadow of the steeple pointed to five.

In the middle of the busy street, Brtko stopped to compare his watch with the steeple clock and then felt free to enjoy the sight of people strolling up and down Main Street; things were getting livelier by the minute.

For a while he watched the carefree boys with their girls in flowered dresses. Then his gaze came to rest on an extraordinary hat; the wearer was taking her little dog for a walk, and the worst of it was that Brtko had forgotten all about his. The lady was incensed: "Keep him on the lead, can't you? Tessie, Tessie darling, come along nicely, now. There's a good girl. Shoo!"

It was nothing but a harmless flirtation, limited on the part of Nugget to a few sniffs and longing glances. Brtko begged pardon in endless apologetic bows and embarrassed smiles, backing helplessly until he hit a stroller. Then, seized by a sudden interest in the curly-headed girl in the baby carriage, he tickled it under the chin, making funny noises and snapping his fingers for his own delight as much as for the mother's. Nugget was at his heels, displaying an equally fascinated interest in a black and white flock of nuns tripping with shy feet hidden beneath full skirts and fingers clasped round their rosaries. Eight of them, two by two, passed along Main Street, and the people made way for these women who had forsworn the delights of this world. Brtko ran a finger round under his collar trying to dig out the curiously uneasy feeling it gave him to think about them.

His carpenter's ear detected in the noise around him the familiar ring of axes, the thud of hammers, and the groan of planes. This clatter so dear to his heart was coming from a timber pyramid soaring up in the middle of the square, an amazing monument to pride and arrogance, its gleaming white tip high above the tops of the chestnut trees round the square.

The pyramid thrust up and up like a white tongue eager to lick the blue paint off the sky. Brtko slapped his knee and whistled through his fingers, for this was one of those moments when he wanted the dog by his side.

Nugget seemed to have decided he'd had enough of waiting for his hesitant master and set out to point the way forward himself. Even so, from time to time he turned to make sure he had not gone too far ahead. Bumping against a soldier's jack boot and rubbing softly against a girl's calf, he sat down on his slim rump and pricked up his ears.

"After him, boys!"

"Come on, let's get 'im!"

They might mean him; he had better be careful. Even Brtko felt in his self-conscious way that they might mean him. In the end it was only a game, the boys showing off in front of their girls. Brtko scratched the dog's ears and put on a determined, decided expression, tossing his head. "Ice cream, ice cream" came from a sunburned fellow in a red fez, pushing his ice-cream cart almost at the double, and furiously ringing the little brass bell tied to the handlebar. "Ice cream! Ice cream!" Then Brtko left behind him the tinkling bell and the hoarse cries of the local Turk.

He walked around the perimeter of the square with careful attention, as though he and his dog had been given a secret mission to record the smallest detail concerning the building of the pyramid. Brtko seemed to be calling on all his powers of invention and his craftsman's skill in order to commit to memory the testimony he would later be called upon to provide. He made a conscientious note of the comings and goings on the building site, considered the breadth of the base and the way each storey was being laid on top of the one below. From this distance, he could not recognize the faces of the men working there, but he could see them impatiently passing beams and planks. Against the white of the scaffolding, they looked like big black ants.

Brtko knew well enough what a job it must be to set up a monster like that. The very proportions of this pyramid suggested a pagan Moloch overwhelming mere man with awe. The carpenter made no secret of his admiration; or was it just the uneasiness that we feel when faced with some mighty exotic creature, incalculable and therefore dangerous, that made him walk more quickly?

He had made a tour of the square and suddenly did not know what to do next. He stretched out a hand toward the pyramid and then, catching the eye of a chimney sweep grinning from ear to ear, pretended to be fumbling with a button. He hesitated, a prey to that feeling of uneasiness again. What was he to do with those hands of his? He looked down at his blistered palms and up at the pyramid and down at his hands again, and in powerless anger he struck out at the dog.

Shocked by this unexpected attack, Nugget growled and bared his teeth at his master. With his tail between his legs he disappeared into the crowd, hurt to the quick.

A great pile of panels lay there, unloaded that very day or perhaps just an hour or so ago. Brtko clambered halfway up, testing the quality of the material, tapping here and there, assessing how hard and seasoned the timber was, measuring the thickness of the panels and breathing in their fine aroma.

Then he called the dog to him.

Nugget did not intend to be dragged away from what he had discovered. It was even a dangerous business, trotting about on that polished slab of marble, and there were many remarkable features to be observed on the stone monument lying overturned under the chestnut tree. There were words cut into the marble:

They gave their lives for freedom
Josef Turna
Mikuláš Gazda
Emil Bruder

His head to one side, the dog seemed to understand what he read. He listened for his master's whistle, and, when he thought he had the direction right, he sat up and begged, waving his paws wildly, as if expecting a reward. What could he expect from the giggling children and indifferent grownups passing by? Nugget lifted a leg and sent a thin stream over the stone, then ended his performance by the overturned slab with a neat jump down. All he cared about now was not to annoy anyone; nose to the ground, he picked up his master's scent and pushed his way through the legs of the throng to where the carpenters' benches stood under the open sky.

It was just at this moment that the crowd parted to make way for an important person: a tall man accompanied by two of the Hlinka guards was approaching from the sidewalk. Catching sight of the man in his freshly pressed uniform, Brtko took an anxious step backwards and mingled with the crowd. He had really come here meaning to meet Marcus Kolkocky and tell him what he thought of him, but he had soon changed his mind. With his hangers-on round him and the crowd about, Marcus Kolkocky was in any case far too busy to notice an insignificant little man in a carpenter's apron. He stretched out his hand and pointed at the tip of the pyramid, looking very pleased with himself. He ran a hand over the scaffolding, slapped the bearded carpenter on the back, and listened to the report made by the foreman, a small fellow in an open-necked shirt. The report on progress seemed to be satisfactory, and Kolkocky was able to proceed to the most important moment in his tour of inspection. He ran up the wooden steps and onto the pyramid, and then he appeared two storeys up and waved to the crowd below. Brtko followed the gaze of the rest of the crowd. He hated Kolkocky and yet he knew the value of what the commander could grant him by a mere wave of his hand. Never, never would he lower himself to ask a favor of this man. Standing here so far below him, Brtko realized that quite clearly, and regret and powerless fury were etched into his features, while the people round him could laugh and take life easy.

TWO

Eveline could not resist unloading herself on her husband; she made no bones about what she thought at the best of times, and why spoil the pleasure of a good row?

"They're all better off than we are," she burst out, and the brevity of her complaint may also have been due to the difficulty of launching into a diatribe kneeling on one knee by the fire. She was loading her iron with red-hot coals.

"It's not a bit of good giving you good advice; you always know better. Why don't you better yourself like Skablo and Petrus and the rest of them? But you wouldn't do something like that, would you? Why don't you find work? That wouldn't be like you, would it? Why don't you whistle to their tune? Think you'd choke on it?"

Now that the iron was as full of coals as it could be, she was free to watch the effect of her words. Her free hand straightened the new print frock under her apron and tried to pull it down to cover her bare knees. Her clothes were tight and narrow and threatening to burst at the seams with the robust vitality of her body. Even the sloppy old slippers seemed too tight for her feet.

She threw the poker into the corner, but not even that clatter roused her husband. There was nothing she could do to disturb his calm, so deeply was he engrossed in what he was doing, and what- she was convinced-was as pointless as everything else he did. The only thing that still mattered to him was getting the last bit of engrained dirt off the cracked washbowl. He was sitting on a bench with the bowl between his knees as though he were soldering a patch on it, but all he was doing was wasting her precious scouring powder, rubbing away obstinately with a bit of rag. She shook a hand in his direction in helpless fury. "What's the use?" And Brtko did not bother to lift his head as he waved in her direction.

"Carry on, carry on in your own way. I don't meddle in your business, and don't you meddle in mine." He went on rubbing the washbowl clean.

"Just you wait, I'll give you meddling!" she raged, and ran out of the kitchen. She did not go far. The iron in her up-raised hand, she paused on the doorstep looking round the yard as though she wanted to light her way across. The dog licked her bare leg in passing and got a kick for his pains. "You filthy cur!" The wind in the branches of the walnut trees drowned his whimper, and his white legs pattered off into the shadows. Eveline clicked the iron shut, checking that it wouldn't fly open, and then the coals, glowing as she swung the iron through the air, blinked through the holes in its sides and carved fiery trajectories through the darkness of a forlorn and run-of-the-mill evening.

She seemed to Brtko to have worked off her anger, and the angry stamping of her feet seemed but the echo of their quarrel; but in fact she was reminding him of her presence.

Tono Brtko looked determined not to notice anything his wife did or said. Standing by the fire, he was scooping warm water into the bowl on the floor, using a little pan. He watched the stream of water falling and splashing in delight, like a child who has discovered something that is not only harmless, but a pleasure as well.

"Stop splashing!" Eveline shouted at him. "You're worse than a kid." Then she gave up; there was no use wasting her breath, and there was enough ironing in the basket to keep her going till midnight.

The stream of water falling from the pan struck the bottom of the bowl and then rose in a geyser of spray and steam. He felt like an artist creating a great work, some-thing that called for passionate concentration and endless patience. He had taken off his boots and tucked his trousers up above his knees, and now he took his jacket off as well. With a tentative finger he tested the heat of the water in the bowl and added a pan of cold. From beginning to end this was a ceremony that could not be carried out in rush and haste but called for conscious enjoyment of measured gestures. Carrying the bowl of water over to the bench, he wiped the floor round it, pulled it nearer to his feet, and threw a wary glance at his wife as he sat down. He wanted to make sure he was going to be allowed to enjoy his foot bath right to the last moment, or else be ready for the attack on his freedom that was being prepared. He was not at all sure. Just as he lifted his feet, Eveline banged the iron down on the upturned saucepan she used as an iron stand, rested her hands on the ironing board like an orator about to address the throng, thrust her imposing bust forward, and held forth:

"No sense, that's what's the matter with you, not a grain of sense. Everybody knows it, it's only you don't know yet that all you have to do is open your great mouth and yell *Support the Hlinka guards!* and they'll come running to help you to your feet. You're the only one who's fool enough to try to stay out of that; you're the fool that doesn't want to know what's going on; you'll never know any better."

She followed it up with one more hopeless sigh. "It was an unlucky hour indeed when the good Lord punished me by tying me to a nincompoop for the rest of my days!"

Brtko had finally decided not to let himself be bothered. Leaning back against the wall with his arms crossed and his feet in the steaming bowl of water, he half closed his eyes and let himself dream that his wife's reproaches were aimed at somebody else, somebody he didn't even know. Warm water has the miraculous power of driving worries away; it was sheer enjoyment, and it washed the poison right out of that insistent voice.

And yet he suddenly spoke to her: "Say, Eveline, d'you know what?" His voice was mild and he looked like a man who has found the answer he wanted at last. Then, as if he had lost his thread, he started fumbling for a cigarette in his jacket pocket, drew the lighted match toward his lips and his eyes widened. At that moment a furious barking outside the house startled him. He lifted his feet out of the water and poised them in mid-air, listening; there was no doubt about it-steps were passing the window and approaching the door.

The two of them looked towards the door as an impatient knocking demanded entrance.

"Come in," Eveline called out, and Brtko blew on his match.

Perhaps it was the shock that did it. Eveline put her iron down, but instead of standing it on the upturned saucepan she used as a stand, she put it on the blanket wrapped around the ironing board. The door swung open, and there stood Marcus Kolkocky, local commander of the Hlinka guards, and his wife, Rose, Eveline Brtko's sister.

The new arrivals stood stock-still, as if stopped in their tracks in a wild dash begun in a moment of folly. Everybody looked embarrassed, taken by surprise and not sure what the outcome of this sudden confrontation was going to be.

Kolkocky's smile, assumed for the occasion, died away. He had expected to be greeted with open arms. Instead, the inexplicable fixity of the pair in the kitchen made an unfortunate impression on him.

Things look very different when a moment of tension makes us see them as others do, and so Eveline's glance as she recovered from her surprise was full of shamefaced excuses. Her eyes roamed from one heap indicating slovenliness to another: the embarrassing poverty of the striped sheets on the unmade bed, the yellowish gleam of the pale electric-light bulb on a row of bottled tomatoes on the kitchen cupboard, the pile of unwashed saucepans in the sink that the newcomers' sharp eyes could not miss. She felt as though the ironing board in front of her was stuck to her body, and, catching sight of her husband with his feet in the washbowl, she would have liked nothing better than to hurl it at him. And the depressing awkwardness of seeing plates licked clean and an overturned saltcellar on the oilcloth of the kitchen table! In those few seconds Eveline registered the elegance and trim superiority of her sister, with the silver-fox fur and the wonderful hat, the discreet gleam of smiling, gold-filled teeth, and the violet velvet dress with its V neck. She was daintily clean and well kept, and glittering with beads and earrings. Hastily, as if she had just remembered it, Eveline tore off her pinafore, and she would have torn off her print dress, too, if she could. Now she could compare the two men, her husband and her sister's, and she could not bear to look at the one sitting there motionless with his shoulders hunched up, looking like a scared tortoise faced with unexpected catastrophe.

If annoyance or a sudden inspiration had not made Brtko splash about in the water with his feet, perhaps Kolkocky would not have burst into that loud laugh of his. He raised his bulging briefcase high above his head in both hands, like a weight lifter triumphantly determined to break all records. "We've come to your rescue! It's high time you pulled yourselves together. Rescue, my dear in-laws, that's what we're after, rescue is what we've brought you!" His voice sounded like a response to people who'd fallen through thin ice and were drowning. The helping hand was stretched out-they had only to catch hold of it.

"Rose, darling! Is it really you? I can't believe my eyes!" Eveline gulped with emotion across the ironing board. Her hands fluttered desperately in the air, eager to wave away the embarrassment between them. "Oh, I'm so terribly glad to see you here."

Her voice grew more convincing as sincerity came to the surface, hope began to glimmer, and dreams that might come true seemed promisingly near.

Rose Kolkocky was not to be outdone in gushing affection. "My dearest little sister! How I'd like you to believe we've never forgotten you for an instant!"

The tapping of high heels grew hurried. The joy of both sisters was underscored by convulsive embraces, broken sobs, shrill squeals, flattering admiration, and mutual assurances that never, never again would anything in the world come between them.

"You're as pretty as ever, Eveline. Every time I caught sight of you I was ashamed we'd let such a trifle come between us . . . I don't know what came over us . . . You haven't changed a bit!"

"You're looking well, yourself, Rose. What a lovely hat! Did you buy it at Imrich's? Let me have a good look at you, now."

As the cries of mutual admiration died down, curiosity rose in its place; they held each other at arm's length, as when the partners in a gypsy folk dance take a good look at each other before whirling round again at an even wilder tempo.

"Before you lose your heads altogether, take a look at this!" Marcus Kolkocky shouted, and started waving his bulging briefcase about again like a railway man trying to stop a hurtling locomotive in the darkness with his lantern. Every movement brought a white shirt cuff peeping out, and a gold watch glittering underneath it-or was it the dazzling sparkle of his diamond rings?

Tono Brtko ran a hand over his sweating forehead, eyes, and face and in his uneasiness tipped his bowl of water over.

The water trickled gaily over the wooden floor in little streams. Marcus Kolkocky's laughter was like a cold shower: "A flood!" he hooted. "A flood! Help, help, we're drowning! Take to the boats!" He hopped about between the puddles on tiptoe, taking care not to splash himself with this miserable poverty, holding up his trouser legs and yelling: "Help! Help! A flood!"

"Mother of God! If that isn't just like him! It's no good my telling him don't wash your feet in the kitchen, don't splash it all about here, don't spill the water, why don't you take it out in the yard. . . . It's no good; whatever you say and whatever you do, it's all the same. . . . Here's a chair; do sit down now, please. I'll have things straight in no time. What a mess!" Eveline clutched her head in her hands, looked round wildly, jumped this way and that, and finally got hold of a bucket and a floorcloth. "Everything will be all right, for heaven's sake sit down and make yourselves at home, won't you?"

Rose clasped her hands in horror, her eyes nearly falling out of her head: "Fire! Look, over there!"

She pointed to the ironing board, where smoke was rising from the folded blanket where the iron rested on it.

Barefoot, Brtko dashed across the kitchen and threw the remaining water in his bowl over the iron. There was a hissing sound and a cloud of steam rose from the cloth, shrouding the others and leaving only their shadowy outlines to be seen jumping about the place; words came through in snatches amidst the coughing.

"Bravo, Tono, bravo! We'll have to put you in charge of the fire brigade!" "Open the door first!"

"We'll be asphyxiated in here!"

"Mind your hair, ladies!"

"Phew, what a stink!"

The hectic laughter, at times spontaneous and at times forced, had gradually died down and receded before a ceremonial which called for dignity if not for admiration. Even their feet below the table were calmer now, except for a pair of bare feet with toes sticking out, rubbing one against the other as if to call each other to order and behave appropriately in the rapidly achieved tidiness of the kitchen and in the presence of such grand guests. There would no longer be any need for Eveline to subdue her radiant smile; her unruly hair had been forced into its bun, and in her new jumper she looked more festive. Her plump hands, lying on the table, were longing to caress all the magnificent gifts. Rose, too, could hardly hide her satisfaction at being the bearer of so much generosity. "I looked after the food and Marcus bought the drinks," she confided cheerfully, putting her hat at a fetching angle.

Brtko was the only one who appeared deep in thought, as if some vital problem was racking his brain; he ran his fingers through his short-cropped hair.

"And it's not just any old stuff to drink either," said Marcus, and brought out of the briefcase on his lap a few more bottles with colourful labels to join the two on the table. "Just take a look at this," he chanted like a conjurer magicking untold riches out of thin air, "just see for yourselves." The bottles passed from hand to hand, and the various labels were duly acknowledged. "French brandy, as in real French brandy from France." Marcus made sure they realized it. "That's the sort of stuff only brass hats get hold of these days. This is cheese from Holland, and that's-"

"Spanish sardines," Rose twittered delightedly, and went on: "We've even brought a bit of butter . . ."

". . . and some sugar and rice and rum," Marcus broke in. We'll drink like sailors getting into port, and drink to our in-laws. May they make their fortune!"

"And think nothing but good of us," Rose added in sentimental tones.

"Let bygones be bygones," Marcus went on, laying food out on the table. "We'll turn over a new leaf; things are looking up. My God, we've never had it so good, and it's only ever going to get better."

The briefcase was empty now and flew in an arc from his hand to the corner of the room.

"Didn't I always say so?" Eveline was moved. "Mark my words, Tono, blood is thicker than water. The good Lord has shown great mercy on our family. He's raised Marcus to high office, and He won't let you go on slaving over your carpenter's bench forever. We've had rough words in the past, but-God willing-we'll make it up again. Look at us now, it's just as I said."

She turned to her husband with sudden determination:

"Get the wedding set out of the cabinet, go on, get a move on- and glasses. Don't forget to wipe them first! I can't even begin to tell you how happy I am . . ."

With her finger to her lips, Rose indicated that a great moment had come. She unfastened the magnificent piece of costume jewelry she wore round her neck, enjoying this opportunity for ostentatious generosity. Getting solemnly to her feet, she put it round her sister's neck and fastened it there, her little fingers raised delicately.

Eveline half closed her eyes in luxurious ecstasy, raising her hands as if to abandon herself completely to this un-heard-of pleasure, letting dreams of wealth unfold behind her lowered lids. She came back to earth as her sister kissed her on both checks. Feeling the trinket between her fingers, she stammered her thanks: "A valuable thing like this . . . what a wonderful present . . . how can we ever repay you?

"What's that? Repay what?" Brtko shouted, but fortunately nobody took any notice of his protests.

The cork popped and drink gurgled into the glasses.

"Let's stand and drink a toast," Marcus Kolkocky suggested.

The glasses clinked in the air above the table, and they all looked at Marcus as he gave an energetic tug at his tie. Clearing his throat, he declared solemnly: "Look at a calf, now, the way it sticks to its mother. Why does a calf stick to its mother? Because of family feeling, that's why.

Here's to our family and may we stick together. To our family!"

"To our family!" they chorused, and drained their glasses. Marcus filled them up again and went on as they raised the liquor to their lips again, "While we're on the subject, let's agree that what's past is past, drowned in brandy and rum and wine, damn it; you'll do fine with us and we'll do better still. To us!"

With the next round he went on: "Third time lucky, brother and sister, that's the way we always drank and that's the way I'll go on drinking. God Almighty, Tono, stop glowering and get the stuff down your throat before I start getting angry and breaking the place up."

This full-speed beginning to the festivities was almost too much for them, and they all sat down with a noisy scraping of chairs. Not all: to the surprise of the others, Tono Brtko stood towering over the table like an ominous portent above the surface of a lake. This moment seemed to him the one he had been waiting for. He took a good look at his companions and felt the need to screw his courage up a bit further. One more drink taken neat and he'd show them, they needn't think he wouldn't. And another one to keep that one company. And a third to cap them both. "A lot of hot air," he grumbled, and downing drinks neat didn't seem to be such a good idea any more. If Eveline hadn't been pulling at his jacket and nagging him to sit down because nobody cared what he thought, anyway, he would have sat down, but, as it was, he had to stay on his feet. He drank again, and they all fell silent.

"Have you gone mad all of a sudden?" Eveline's voice was pregnant with menace.

"I'm thirsty. This is the medicine for me." It was the best answer he could have given, and now he could sit down.

"Tono's just like a kid-you could tell from his face he'd got something on his mind," Rose twittered amiably.

Her comment encouraged Brtko to get to his feet again, but his wife thrust him back into his seat.

"Let him have his say," Marcus interceded.

Tono was taken aback by his brother-in-law's good will.

"Time enough," he said nonchalantly, and waved a vague hand. "I saw you today, on that . . . precious tower of yours, the devil take it. . ."

"I'd be with you every evening. . ."

Eveline began to sing, to cover up the awkward moment; the others joined in:

If you'd only give me
What I want to get
I'd like a dashing devil
With eyes as black as jet . . .

At length even Brtko tried to add his voice to theirs, but all he could get out was a curious creaking sound. He could not dissemble or overcome his scorn and dislike of his brother-in-law. He got up again and waved a hand to get silence. "Pipe down, woman," he growled at Eveline when she tried to stop him.

"Let him have his way, Eveline, he's just like a baby." Rose took his side.

Brtko had lost all self-restraint. His hatred was ready to burst out with no thought for the consequences, and even Kolkocky had to lower his eyes before that scornful gaze. Marcus settled himself more comfortably in his chair, rested his head in his hands, and pretended interest in what Brtko was going to say. He even encouraged him to get going: "You've got the floor, Tono, go ahead. We're all listening to what you've got to say."

"I've got the floor whether you give it to me or not." Tono's voice still seemed to be held in check. "Wonderful presents you've brought us, haven't you? Generous gifts, lots of stuff . . . but what about our share of the inheritance, eh? You generous benefactors, you, what've you got to say about that? Ah-ha!! You bribed the tax man, that's as clear as daylight, and you shut the mouth of the notary from the land registry with money, too, didn't you, so as you could pinch the ground from under our feet and the roof from over our heads, and what about the bees, I say, what about the swarm? Died on me, they did, the very next spring. . . . And what was it you said when I came to ask for a job on that Tower of Babel you've built yourself in the square, eh? What sort of a song were you singing then, eh? I've got better and cheaper carpenters than you, that's what you said, wasn't it? What have you got to say for yourself now, eh?"

"I'll call the next tune," Marcus yelled, "and make it a rousing one, a real folk dance, something to keep that mouth of yours busy!" And he snapped his fingers in time to the tune.

Eveline seized anxiously on the chance to finish the argument without a fight, and Rose joined in the chorus:

"Better to be poor and good;
Let the world run as it should."

Brtko was waving his arms in the air wildly, protesting at the injustice done to him; he stamped and banged on the table and wanted an answer to his questions. They were holding justice up to scorn, and he felt like a child left alone in a blazing barn. "Shame on you, shame on you," he was shouting, "why don't you answer me if you're as clever as you make out? Now's the time to be talking, now!"

They did not want to hear him, shouting the song at the tops of their voices to drown his importunate and persistent nagging. They did not stop their noise until Marcus waved a hand for silence and said:

"Bygones are bygones, Tono, aren't they? We're all one happy family, aren't we? Let's have another round—a round of brandy this time."

"Brandy! Brandy!" the women shrieked, and Eveline jumped up to take the bottle, anxious to help Marcus to dispel the threatening clouds of dissension. In her excitement she spilled a drop, letting the glass fill too full, and Rose squealed excitedly: "Oh, look, there's going to be a christening—Eveline's going to have a baby!"

"It'd better be twins," chortled Marcus, "to make up for lost time."

"I'm too old for that sort of thing." Eveline tried to look prim and handed the first glass to her husband. "You'd better come to your senses, you old windbag."

"I'll not touch another drop until I've heard the truth!" And Tono angrily pushed his wife's hand away, drink and all.

The atmosphere was getting tense again, and Marcus yelled:

"I'll give you carpenters, you loud-mouthed trouble-maker." He rose threateningly in his chair, holding on to the arms with both hands. "Just you listen to me, you aborted grub, you! Do you know where I could be today if it weren't for you? All because you wouldn't join the guards? An alibi man, that's what they think I am—d'you know what that means? Getting myself an alibi, in case . . .? You . . . you . . . more Ali Baba than Alibi. Ha ha!"

He took another drink to wash away his anger with the pun he was so proud of, and went on in a friendlier tone: "Now just let's get this straight once and for all. . . . Birds of a feather and all that . . . may I drop dead on the spot if I didn't come here just to do you a good turn, Tono. Don't worry; I'll make up for that inheritance of yours over and over again, if you just listen to me like the gospel, as sure as my name's Kolkocky," and he banged on the table to lend emphasis to his words: "I've made you the Aryanizer of old Lautman's shop. . . What d'you say to that, eh? Here's the license for you—now d'you believe me?"

He fished a piece of paper out of his pocket and flung it in Brtko's face, wiping the sweat from his cheeks as if the performance had been too much for him.

Eveline's voice rose ecstatically. "I knew it! I knew it! I swear I knew something like that was in the air, all along!" And with a tipsy cackle she flung herself into her brother-in-law's arms.

Holding her firmly in his lap Marcus began another song:

I've got a wonderful girl all the same,
A girl with a wonderful shop to her name;
She sells tatties, tatties, tatties. . .

"Who's talking about tatties?" Eveline was in high spirits now, waving her hands about in time to the song. "We'll have better-class stuff than *that* to sell."

The women hurried over to the stove to prepare a bite of something to eat; Brtko was still gripping his glass tight. He could crush it if he tried; he had only to close his fist tighter round it and it'd be in splinters. It's a funny view of the world you get through a glass, all changed, narrowed, distorted, and yet so clear he thought he could hit a target like the monstrous head beyond the table, the head that belonged to Marcus. Brtko closed one eye to take aim and felt he was pressing a trigger. A flame flashed at the point where his target was; the blinding gleam of his brother-in-law's jeweled cigarette case took his breath away. As if he had read Brtko's thoughts, Kolkocky said: "Don't worry, you'll soon have made your little packet, too."

"It's an easy life, isn't it?"

"Who said easy? Whose life are you talking about, anyway?"

"As I said. It's an easy life for swindlers."

"Who do you mean by that?"

"D'you think I mean the few decent men who haven't dirtied their hands?"

Kolkocky thrust his hand out, palm upward, and Tono seemed to see a handful of grain.

"Take a peck, now, do take a peck," Rose twittered by the stove, holding a canapé to her sister's lips.

"I'm a bit peckish myself," Brtko answered, as though the words had been meant for him, for his eyes were still fixed on Kolkocky's hand.

"How can you tell whether the grain's poisoned or not?" he thought aloud. "There's plenty of people have grown fat at the Aryanization trough, as fat as pigs; but I've a feeling it might make me sick."

"There you go, brother, drunk as a skunk, that's the way you are." Marcus waved him away with a shrug.

"Come on, now, you're the reason for the celebration round here; you'd better get your strength up again," Rose chirped, bringing him down to earth again and popping a sardine in his mouth as he opened it, which made the others laugh.

"You're a fine one, feeding my hero like a baby." Eveline pretended to be angry.

"Don't expect too much of him all at once. It takes time to get used to living like the rich. I remember when we first . . ." They sat down at the table again. "And it's not so long ago," Rose went on with her tale, "my beast of a doctor forbade me to smoke. Just think of that—not a single cigarette!"

Eveline could not get over her amazement. "What did you do?"

"I'm going to have one just to spite him. Why don't you light up, too? Come on, have a cigarette," and she turned to her sister and Tono. Marcus put cigarettes between their lips for them and brought out his expensive lighter with a flourish.

They all puffed away and felt terribly important, like mischievous children enjoying a forbidden game. Soon the cloud of cigarette smoke enveloped them; they fell silent from sheer tiredness, and into the dumb murkiness the wooden cuckoo spoke from the clock on the wall.

"Time for a drink," Kolkocky shouted. "Let's drink to our good fortune. One for the road!"

The glasses gleamed as they were raised and lowered, a ceremony repeated many times until the tinkling grew wilder and the eyes burned and laughter came in ragged snatches. They were determined to drink themselves under the table.

The rows of bottles on the floor grew and grew; their words became wilder and wilder, hair disordered; a lady's hat flew through the air to land on the striped bed cover, the diamond-studded cigarette case felt cool to Tono's toes under the table, a tie with a gold tiepin was draped over the edge of the sink among the dirty dishes. The cuckoo thrust its beak into the smoke and called midnight.

"To-no, To-no, To-no, To-no," they were clapping in time to their hoarse voices, and Tono Brtko, his eyes staring, his hips twisting convulsively, stepped back from the table and said in a loud voice with no attempt to hide his ridicule:

"As the ladies and gentlemen wish. . . . What's the difference between a poor man and a monkey? If you like I'll do more than drink—I'll be your fool as long as you ask for it."

"Hooray!"

"Bravo!"

There was silence for a second. Tono gave another look at the company driving him on to show what he could do, and then the glasses started toward him in a chain. He tipped them down his throat one after the other, and the others watched tense and silent as the contents of twelve glasses gurgled down. As the last disappeared, Rose called out dreamily:

"Isn't he just spectacular?"

"Bravo, Tono!"

"Hooray! Hip, hip, hooray!" Their applause was a little embarrassed and a little relieved, but Tono was not going to allow their drunken admiration to flag. He dashed the last glass to the floor, and with one leap, he landed on the table.

Barefoot and in his shirt sleeves, with his trousers rolled up to his knees, he towered over them looking down on their tousled hair and flushed faces; he felt like a peddler at a fair, wiser than the fools listening to him with admiration. He spat on his hands and flung his arms wide to ask for silence; then with the wild determination of a drunken man and with a hitherto unsuspected energy, he held two fingers on his upper lip and shouted: "The Führer is going to speak! Silence for the Führer!" Then he barked rapidly: *"Vanvilich, veinen, veinsinige!"* He followed it up with eyes rolling ecstatically and convulsive jerks of his body, imitating Hitler making a speech; the onlookers watched in awe and admiration. Angry scraps of incomprehensible words were spewed from his lips: *"Undzunach, undendredfuhr, brotrot, glukvernichtamal herrgott beidenvollen—folendrunknicht, ibeljubel firends, hinaus, fermeshausmaschinen lassen hipheil, hipheil, hipheill."*

As he finished he looked exhausted and quite sober. His eyes were glowing with scorn. Kolkocky was so moved by what he had heard that he shot his arm out in the Hitler salute as the orator concluded, and shouted in all seriousness: *"Sieg Heil!"*

"Geil! Geil!" Tono repeated mockingly, and jumped down to the floor.

"Isn't he fun?" Rose called in delight, but Tono heard nothing and saw nothing. His hands to his mouth, he wanted to get rid of the awful taste on his tongue, but all at once he did not know which way to go, whether to dash for the yard or not to risk it and make for the washbowl. Everything began revolving round him, and the sour flood caught up with him. Stumbling, he fell full length on the floor. They all stood frozen to the spot and watched drunkenly as he raised himself on one elbow and looked first at the mess in front of him and then at them. Hoarse and carefully chewing each syllable, he addressed them: "What the hell do you think you're looking at? Never seen a drunk before? Look at the snakes here . . . right here . . . under my nose . . . your world seen in a mirror . . ."

The sight of the filth spreading over the floor in front of him so angered him that he slapped his hand down in it, and they jumped away as if it were an evil omen. Rose crossed herself hastily. Eveline came to herself and rushed at her husband with fists clenched and all her energy to spare.

"Let me get at him, just let me get at the swine . . . the foul beast . . . the sot . . . I'll show him!"

The blows rained down on him, and a resigned grimace flitted over his face. As Eveline's arms began to flag he muttered: "Feeling better now? I've never felt worse . . ."

Kolkocky sighed and put on a moralizing tone. "That's the way it always is. You do your best to help him, and there he is, rolling about in his own filth like a . . . like a swine." He hiccoughed. "Excuse the language . . ."

Brtko dragged himself over to the bed and fell onto the striped cover. It was more than Rose could do to get her hat on straight.

THREE

Eveline had washed to the waist and rubbed herself dry; she still had to tidy her things away and do her long black hair; it fell down over her bare shoulders. She whistled and hummed, longing for someone to talk to, and there was Tono fast asleep as though this was just another ordinary day, instead of being practically a feast day. She had brought in two pails of water from the well, the fire was burning merrily in the stove, and all she had to do was to grind a handful of coffee. She felt so restless that she would have liked to move the hands of the clock forward.

The brassy sound of the coffee grinder entered Brtko's dream in the form of bells playing a tune. "Who's there?" he asked at the door of the gingerbread cottage.

"It's me," replied Eveline happily as she carried the grinder over to the door.

"You look strange," said Tono, still half asleep.

Washed and neat, in a flowered dress with full gathered sleeves, she reminded him of an enormous exotic butterfly.

"Are you getting ready for a fancy-dress ball?" he asked.

"I'm a new woman today." Eveline was bubbling over. "I'm so happy. Do get up! Come on! I had to go beyond the bridge for the milk this morning; just imagine, Andras's piebald was in calf, and it was born dead. Did you have a good sleep? I didn't get a wink all night . . . ."

The clatter of the brass mill turned into a tolling bell.

"What do you think I'm getting ready for you?"

"A coffin," he murmured sleepily.

"Are you still asleep?"

"I dreamed I saw a white butterfly."

"That means luck, a lucky white butterfly, a white flag, neighborly charity . . ."

He couldn't get used to her amiability and had to sit up and put his feet on the floor before he felt really awake. He yawned and stretched.

"Oh, those poor little creatures." She flew to the door with milk in a little pan. "I forgot all about them." With a newly-acquired smile she watched the black tomcat carefully approaching the dog with a pleading gaze.

"Good morning to you, neighbor," the one-armed tobacconist called out on his way to the shop. "You're up bright and early this morning, aren't you?"

"That's right, we're nice and early," she repeated, and hurried back indoors without really answering him.

"Three years I've been saving this pot of honey." She simpered at her husband sitting at the table. "I swore we wouldn't touch it until we'd made it up with Marcus and Rose. Do you remember the day they brought it? Just think of it . . . the whole town will be talking about us now . . . it was they who came here in the end. They need us just as much as we need them."

The honey was dripping from the spoon onto the slice of bread—clear, scented, blessed honey; it would be a shame to lose a single drop.

The cups on the table were steaming. Brtko sat there in his under shirt; he hadn't even managed to put his suspenders on. He had to satisfy his hunger first. Eveline was sitting at the table, too; it had been a long time since they had had breakfast together like this. The dog barked outside.

It's not easy to make a dog see that cats are friends. The moment the tomcat had finished the milk, he had lost all interest in his pal and refused to play. He felt much safer up in the walnut tree, while the dog stood there with his muzzle in the air, threatening revenge.

The clothes brush was part of the festive morning; Eveline wouldn't have him go off with a speck of dirt or a morsel of fluff on his best suit. "I'm not letting you go off to your own shop looking like a beggar."

Tono thought that the yard, right in front of the door, was not a suitable place for all this. "Stop it, for heaven's sake." He tried to fend her off. "I'm not a kid."

"You're worse than a child half the time. Don't you forget that from now on you own a shop. Do you think I'm letting you go there in muddy boots? You must be mad!"

"You don't have to do this where everybody can see us," he protested.

"Why not? It's nothing to be ashamed of, is it? Everybody's going to envy us now, don't you see!"

It was no good Brtko's trying to hide one foot behind the other; it was no good trying to get away from her and leave the way he'd like to, just slipping out of the yard; Eveline hadn't half finished with him yet. She brushed him in front and she brushed him behind, and then she took his hat and spat on the brush.

Unfortunately, another of the neighbors came across the yard just then, a potbellied, bald-headed fellow whose meerschaum pipe reached down to his belly button. "It was late when your party broke up, wasn't it? Good morning to you!"

"Morning to you, Mr. Piti." Brtko wished the ground would open and swallow him up. It was the worst that could happen—for this old gossip to see him like that. He'd have it round the town in no time. There he was, looking at him like a monkey in a cage.

"Tono, you look just like a bridegroom escaped from the altar at the last minute! What are you dressing him up for, Eveline, the wedding feast?"

"No wedding, no feast—right to Paradise he's going." Brtko's wife added her own little joke.

"I heard the goings on, couldn't help hearing—didn't get much sleep last night. What time might it have been when they went home, now?"

"Who knows," the carpenter muttered, and the man shuffled away.

Brtko felt worse and worse; his best suit was tight and his collar and tie seemed to be strangling him. He felt all wrong wearing a hat, and Eveline kept plying him with good advice:

"Now, mind you, don't let anybody cheat you. You know what people are like. No credit for anyone, either, mind. The man isn't living who can afford to give things away, and money begets money. It wouldn't do any harm to have a motto up on the wall like old Hole did in his pub, 'No penny, no paternoster' or something. . . . Get out!" That was meant for the dog, which kept getting in the way of her feet.

Brtko had gone. There was no use in Nugget's putting his head out of his kennel and whimpering. There was nothing left but the wind swinging the gate to and fro on its hinges.

FOUR

A tinkle overhead startled Brtko as he went through the door and made him twist round to look up at the gadget. "What the . . . what do they want with a bell up there? Newfangled notions . . ." he muttered to himself.

He kept opening and closing the door. He simply had to try it out again and again, stopping to play with it as a child will with a newly discovered toy. . He stood in the doorway for a moment, his head thrown back, and considered the practical value of the gadget. Then he stepped back into the street and compared the wording of his Aryanizer's license with the sign over the shop, ROSALIE LAUTMAN, WIDOW-BUTTONS, LACES, RIBBONS, to be sure he had come to the right place.

"Useless contraption—no point in it here at all!" His finger jabbed a final verdict in the direction of the bell. Not until he had gone down the steps right into the shop, did he realize his judgment had been premature. Carefully, on tiptoe, as though afraid of waking somebody up for no good reason, he took one step at a time forward into the darkness until his eyes grew used to it. In the shadows beyond the counter he thought he could make out the bent figure of an old woman, motionless as a ghost in repose. He cleared his throat, and something stirred and rustled as though the sound had wakened a sleeping owl.

Rosalie Lautman was sure it was her rheumatics that had wakened her, as usual. She suffered from other, less serious troubles of old age, too, so that there was little room left in her mind for what was going on in the town or in the world at large. She needed all her concentration for straightening her painful knuckles. There were days when it gave her a lot of trouble to bend them at all, and, once she had managed that, it took a long time to straighten them out again. At last she asked with lively interest, "What might the young gentleman be looking for?"

It was not often she had the honor to serve a gentleman obviously dressed in his best; he deserved her most respectful attention, and so she rose to her feet behind the counter. But she had not yet worked quite free of her own private troubles, and had to keep rubbing the fingers of her left hand with the palm of her right hand to bring them back to life. Thinking her customer's attentive gaze showed his way of sympathizing with her trouble, she confided in him with the ready communicativeness of old age: "The young gentleman isn't troubled with the rheumatics, I dare say . . . such a nasty thing to have. My fingers are like icicles all day long . . . the doctor said it was gout. 'Not gout, Doctor,' I said, 'old age, that's what it is, old age coming into its own . . .'"

Brtko was genuinely sorry for the old lady. "That's nothing . . . you ought to have seen old Sekerák. Not the ice-cream man, his brother—the one who used to dig ice. You should have seen the way that one looked. See—that's what his fingers were like . . . all twisted and knotted with gout." Brtko gave a feeling and realistic imitation of the sufferer's plight.

"All twisted up like that? You don't say! Dear, dear . . . the poor creature," the old lady lamented, although all she had understood from his gestures was the pain of knotted limbs. No more than that. For years she had had to rely on her eyes alone, for her hearing had long since ceased to serve her. She did not take her eyes off the speaker's lips and gestures, especially when she felt the occasion was an important one. This time she had realized at once that she was talking to a well-brought-up young man. "What did you say the lady's name was?"

She ought not to have given way to her curiosity; it irritated Brtko quite unnecessarily. He began shouting: "It wasn't a woman, for heaven's sake . . . Sekerák, not the ice-cream man though. His brother—the iceman."

"So that's the way it was!" She nodded sympathetically, one forefinger crooked against her upper lip 'Uh Huh.'

"All his life long he ate nothing but salt herrings and now and again dumplings on Sunday. Dumplings with poppy seed and sometimes with a bit of jam. Dumplings!" He raised his voice.

"Now I say there's nothing to beat stuffed fish on the Sabbath." The old lady's voice was almost greedy; she was delighted that chance had brought her so pleasant a companion, so sympathetic to her little pleasures and her troubles alike. She chattered on: "It's really not at all expensive. Just one egg," she counted the ingredients off on her fingers, "or two eggs if it's to feed more people, but one egg is more than enough for me . . . or you can use a drop of milk instead, and if you don't happen to have milk you can make do with water . . . a couple of spoonfuls of flour and a handful of bread crumbs . . . you don't even need teeth, it simply melts on your tongue . . . a real delicacy. Some people like it best with a savoury sauce and some prefer it sweet. I had to remind Imre—he's not as young as he was and he's inclined to be forgetful—Imre, I said, don't forget that bottle of vinegar . . ."

Running on like this, she began to realize that her visitor was not with her.

"That's all right, let's drop it," Brtko said apologetically, and rubbed his hands. "I . . . er . . . I've been made your Aryanizer, as they say . . ." and he thrust his hand deep into his pocket to fish out the license.

The old lady moved her head forward a little and watched his lips closely; there seemed to be something she had missed. "I beg your pardon?" She cupped her ear in her hand.

"I've been given the job of Aryanizing this blasted—er, blessed business," he declared heavily, thinking it would be child's play to come to an agreement with the talkative old lady.

The old lady's eyes were on her customer's lips, and her heart was warmed by such a succession of "b's."

"Buttons!" she cried joyfully, and started bustling about, pulling out boxes and spilling their contents on the counter. "Buttons, of course! Now what kind will the young gentleman be wanting? Big, small, pearl buttons, colored ones, polished or plain, we have a very large selection indeed."

Box after box came down from the shelves and onto the counter. The old lady displayed them before him one after the other, tipping their contents out as he stood there dumbfounded. She did not look straight at him; it is not wise to look at the hands that are making their choice. That must be left to the customer; but she could not help having her say: "There's no relying on a gentleman's taste, I always say. If the young gentleman asks my advice, now, these would go well with a light suit . . . no, no, these would be better, a softer shade of gray. . . The young gentleman doesn't happen to have a scrap of the material with him? No, I thought as much, just like a man."

The silent customer did not seem to be satisfied, and the old lady felt called upon to explain the true state of affairs: "I'm afraid supplies haven't been coming in as they should lately. . . I *have* heard say there's a war on. Nothing Imre does seems to be any help. Poor man, the trouble he takes . . ."

"Mrs. Lautman!" Brtko's patience was running low. Perhaps it wasn't going to be so easy to come to terms with the deaf old creature after all. He set about explaining things in his own way, in a loud, impassioned voice. "I've been made your Aryanizer. That means, you see, that I'm your Aryan and you're my Jewess. Because you're Jewish you've got to be Aryanized and that means I'm Aryanizing you and your business. See? From now on this shop belongs to me and I've got it all down here in black and white. *Now* do you understand?"

Engrossed in his own explanation, he did not notice the old lady's worried expression; there was something she had not understood and could not understand. Her hands dropped helplessly to her sides, and, raising her head, she tried to smile at him.

In the split second between the explanation and its failure to get home, he caught sight of her face through the holes in the button he was pressing to his eye like a monocle, a face crisscrossed by deep lines and the tiny waves of innumerable wrinkles; a hairy wart above the left corner of the mouth looked like a dead spider, belly turned up. Only her eyes indicated that there was still some life left in the old woman. Brtko rapped on the counter with the button he held between his fingers.

"Here it is, all in black and white," he said firmly, pushing the license over the counter toward her. "Just take a look at that." He might have been offering her a box of chocolates or a generous gift.

The old lady's interest quickened visibly at this advance. It was a long, long time since anybody had gone out of his way to entertain her.

"The young gentleman is so amusing," she said kindly. "What has the young gentleman brought me this morning?" Her hand trembled as her long-sighted eyes tried to decipher the joke hidden behind what was written on the sheet of paper.

"Oh, most interesting, most interesting indeed." She nodded affably; then, not quite sure she had not made a mistake, yet proud at not having been forgotten, she ventured to add: "Is the young gentleman from the bailiff's office, perhaps?"

"What does a bailiff have to do with it? Aryanization, that's what I'm talking about."

"Now I thought to myself the minute I set eyes on you- such a nice-mannered young gentleman, I thought. It's very kind of you, it really is. . . . Imre is so conscientious it's almost a fault. Thirty years now he's been taking care of my accounts and all my tax returns . . . he brings me a fish for the Sabbath, every Friday as regular as clockwork—dace or whiting, even a carp now and again. Such a reliable man, a good friend of my dead husband's, and most correct . . . a heart of gold," she ended, pushing the license back across the counter to Brtko. "You must forgive an old woman, my hearing's not what it was. . . . How old will the young gentleman be, now? Not forty yet, I'll be bound. Oh, dear, dear . . . I've got two daughters myself, you know—won't the young gentleman take a seat?—Pretty as a picture, both of them . . . Clarica and Pirica . . . and my poor dear Heinrich . . . well, well, what's past is past. . . What did the young gentleman say his name was? I beg your pardon? Ah, of course, Mr. Batko. A most unusual name . . . do sit down, Mr. Batko. . . Do you come from these parts, Mr. Batko?"

"I'm not Batko—Brtko's the name, Tono Brtko!"

"Well, well, who would have thought it? They grow up so quickly and everything changes as the years go by . . . they get married . . . leave home . . . I don't get about much these days, but I don't really mind. The young gentleman may find it hard to believe me, but the world has changed so much, so very, very much . . ."

An elderly man stepped down into the shop with an agile step; tall and broad-shouldered, he held his shaven head with dignity. He moved with a brisk military step, but his face was kind; there was an angler's creel dangling against his waterproof. With a wink at Brtko, he greeted the old lady.

"Good morning, Rosalie." Leaning his stick against the counter, he stretched his arms wide. The old lady followed his pantomime with friendly interest, although she knew his story by heart.

The angler was getting into his stride: "Just imagine the size of it! . . . that big . . . a pike it was. My heart rejoiced, Rosalie, my soul was filled with delight . . . but when I looked into its eyes—by all that's sacred, I don't think there's any of God's creatures can look as soulful as that fish did. Never be hard of heart, says I, and off with her, back into the water, back you go, my beauty . . ."

"Imre," Mrs. Lautman's voice was beseeching, "we're keeping Mr. Batko waiting . . ."

"Oh, dear me, we mustn't do that. How do you do, Mr. Batko? The old lady isn't far from the mark is she, Batko the Bloodsucker? A carpenter you may be, but there isn't much of the Christlike in you, is there? Well, you rascal, I'm sure we can make some arrangement, can't we?"

The old lady was delighted to find her judgment confirmed; it comforted her to see her old friend being so affable to her visitor. The fisherman flung his arms round the shoulders of the well-dressed gentleman and hugged him like a long-lost brother. The old woman quietly rejoiced at the chance to play the hostess. Let the menfolk swap their stories while she puts some tea on for them in the kitchen.

"Now don't start getting in a temper, Brtko," he spoke softly as the other frowned. "It's not my fault you've come fishing in barren waters. . ."

"What do you mean by that, Mr. Kucharsky? Is this supposed to be a joke? I don't know what you're talking about."

"I'll soon make that quite clear." The older man lowered his voice. "In the first place, just get this into your head: you'll never get rich fishing in *this* pond."

"Who said I wanted to get rich?"

"What are you pushing your nose in here for then?" The older man's voice was sterner than he intended, and to soften the effect of his anger he went on more gently: "I'm glad, really, that you've come in to Aryanize her, and not one of those swine."

"Exactly what are you talking about, Mr. Kucharsky? It seems to me you're poking your nose into things that don't concern you."

"That's just where you're wrong, my dear fellow!" He wagged a finger. "It's true I don't own shares in this business, but in a manner of speaking I do have a stake here . . ."

"I've got a license to Aryanize this place and from now on it belongs to me!"

"Now keep your hair on, Brtko; I'm not taking your license off you. Look here: you're not a bad chap; you're not even a member of the Hlinka guards. I think you ought to take a different line . . ."

"What are you getting at, Mr. Kucharsky? What do you want?"

"Don't worry; I don't want anything off you. I only want to warn you that you've swallowed a foolish bait. They've put something over on you."

"On me? You mind what you're saying. D'you think I'm going to stand here and let a man like you provoke me? I ought to throw you out of here . . . you've no business hanging round this place at all. I could inform on you, that I could! And I will, too. You're a bolshie, that's what you are, and don't think I don't know it."

"Don't get so het up, Brtko, it's bad for you. Has it ever entered your thick head that old Mrs. Lautman couldn't live on what she makes by selling buttons?"

Brtko raised his head, uncomprehending.

"Just think for a moment. Have a good look at what they've let you Aryanize. . . Look here—mildew, cobwebs, empty boxes . . . go on, take a good look at these old shelves and the paint falling off the ceiling and all the rubbish lying around reeking of rot. That's pricked your bubble, hasn't it? And a deaf old Jewess thrown in. The big shots have taken all the prosperous shops themselves; don't you worry about them. Kolkocky wasn't out to make *your* fortune, my lad. They've pulled a fast one on you, that's what."

Brtko's hesitation became a shade more determined. He took one step toward the door.

"Hold on, Brtko!"

The carpenter paused irresolutely. "I'll go and ask him about it."

"Who are you going to ask about what?"

"And if that's the way things are he can have his license back. He can stuff it up his jumper." His voice started to rise. "Just let him try cheating an honest carpenter!" He was shouting, now. "Good morning, Mr. Kucharsky!" He made a second attempt to move.

"Now, just keep your hair on, Tono. Don't you know your own brother-in-law by now? Do you seriously mean to go and reproach him for having taken a first-class store for himself and left you with a useless hole? Don't you know that wouldn't do you any good and could be a very dangerous thing to do?"

"What am I to do, then?" Brtko asked helplessly.

"Nothing. Just leave it to me. Now sit down and listen."

Brtko did as he was told, while the fisherman walked up and down the little shop, explaining the situation. "First of all, as I said before, old Rosalie doesn't live on what she makes on buttons, and hasn't for years. The Jews support her as best they can on charity. . . Sit down, I tell you, things aren't as bad as all that. You won't lose on the deal. Their charity will have to stump up a bit more, that's all. Katz the barber will see to that and you—"

"What about me?" asked the carpenter.

"You'll just leave the old lady alone. That's all. You'll even make a bit on it. What d'you say to that?"

Brtko did not answer.

Kucharsky spat on his hands, spread a piece of newspaper on the counter, and tipped the fish out of his creel.

"Come along, Rosalie, and choose one for the Sabbath," he called with the kindness of a donor anxious to please. He watched as the old lady hobbled in from the kitchen with a tray and put it down on the counter to feel the fish, one by one. Then she finally made up her mind.

"Why take the smallest of the lot?" he cried, and the only response the old lady made to such generosity was an affectionate glance.

"Come along, Tono, and choose one for the Sabbath, too, now you're regent of this Jewish kingdom. You might just as well take something home to make your wife happy as well."

Brtko did not wait to be asked twice.

With polite little gestures the old lady drew the men's attention to the tea on the tray. "Come along and drink it up while it's hot, now," she said in a motherly manner.

She stood behind the counter and the men in front, sipping their tea slowly and savoring the idyllic moment. The older man kept his eyes on the widow without seeming to watch her. Taking advantage of what seemed to be a favorable moment, he downed his tea in two gulps, banged his cup down, and wiped his mouth on his hand. In joyous haste, like a peddler calling his wares, he said very loudly: "Well, now, Rosalie, things couldn't have turned out better." The old woman seemed to sense what was coming as she watched her friend telling her the good news. "This is the way things are, Rosalie; this gentleman, that's right, this fine noble spirit, as you have guessed, is the very man we've been talking about. He has agreed to come and help you in the shop. He'll be around for a month or two, as long as you need him. You needn't worry any more."

The fisherman picked his cup up, buried his nose in it as though licking the sugar off the bottom, and watched the old lady over the rim. Her face was glowing with sincere gratitude. She crossed her arms on her breast as though in prayer. "I always knew you were goodhearted, Imre; you always were kind to me . . . Why deny it? I'm old and I need somebody to help me . . . God bless you."

She gave a little shiver, rearranged her shawl on her shoulders, and shuffled round from behind the counter to stand before them, bowing slightly to these men who were so solicitous about her welfare. She put one foot forward in its old-fashioned buckled boot, uncertain whom to thank first.

"We are never left really alone in the world, though we may fear so at times," she said trustingly. Then, more to the point, "What is the young gentleman's Christian name?"

"He's Tono," Kucharsky shouted the name, "Lily's cousin."

The old lady bent her head on one side. "So that's it," she said, as if everything were now quite clear. Her moist eyes gleamed happily as she gazed at her new assistant. She came up to him and felt for his hand with trembling fingers. "You will be like a son to me," she whispered, and stroked the thunderstruck Tono's sleeve.

"Why, if I wasn't forgetting your vinegar, Rosalie!" And the fisherman drew a bottle out of his creel.

FIVE

Saturday was to be surprisingly eventful for Brtko. He had become a shop assistant without even having had time to accept or refuse the job, and without even stopping to think why he had listened so attentively to a talkative old woman. The following morning he had hurried off to the shop early.

The cows were just emerging from yard gates, standing obediently in front of the cottages and lifting their heads towards the sound of the herdsman's horn. Its clear note drove the last scrap of night out of the farmers' eyes. They came into the street in their underwear, with slippers hastily thrust on or even barefoot, driving their cattle before them as if they had just jumped straight out of bed into the cowshed. The sun was blazing hot even first thing in the morning. Brtko stopped in front of the milking plant. He watched the two farmhands offloading cans with milk. He wasn't in any hurry and he had got through the worst part of the business.

Brtko had disappeared the day before soon after the fisherman, leaving his fish lying on the counter wrapped in its piece of newspaper. The old woman had made him a cup of coffee and had wanted to give him a bite to eat, but he said he had to go home and change first. He did not go back to the shop yet did not dare to go home; it would have looked queer to wander about the streets in his Sunday best, with collar and tie on and a hat that looked almost good enough for a bishop. He would have looked equally out of place at the inn—and what could he have said when they started asking what he was all dressed up for? They would have made fun of him, and that was something Brtko could not stand. Anyway, he had become involved in the sort of thing nobody would approve of who hadn't got mixed up in it themselves.

He found himself down by the river; here, hidden among the bushes, he could enjoy the pleasures of solitude and pretend that nothing really bad had happened.

He took off his boots and all his finery and paddled about in the water in his underpants. Then he lay down, fell asleep, and dreamed silly dreams. After swimming back and forth across the river a few times he felt refreshed, as though he had washed away the musty aftertaste the old lady and her shop had left in his mouth. He no longer bothered his head about what was going to happen next morning.

Only when the shadows began to lengthen across the river did he sit up, pleasantly excited although he did not know why. Hurriedly, as though someone had ordered him to do so, he pulled the Aryanization license out of his coat pocket and read it through. Then he weighted the piece of paper with a stone; at last he knew what he was going to do. He imagined what his own name plate would look like over the shop, drawing an oblong in the sand with a twig. It was a most successful oblong. A mad hope, perhaps roused by the pleasant rest he had enjoyed, brought to the surface of his mind the thought that something might be made of the shop after all.

Later on, sitting at home with his feet in the bowl of steaming water, he let his tongue run on:

"It's a lot of hard work, Aryanizing a shop, Eveline, I can tell you that. . . The old Lautman woman came clean. It doesn't matter,' she said, 'what Tom, Dick or Harry they send in to Aryanize me.' She's going to help me till I get my bearings . . . be my assistant. . . You know what I think, Eveline?"

"Out with it, out with it!"

"The way I look at it, a shop is like a cow. A cow's got to have hay, and a shop's got to have money. If you put money into a shop the gold'll come streaming out like milk from a good milker."

"That's all very well—when are we going to get it? When?"

"Maybe next week. Maybe tomorrow—maybe not till next month. Watch me!" He invited his wife's attention, throwing his arms about and putting on a pitiful grimace. He spoke with the thickened voice of the deaf old woman: "'I'm an old woman, Mr. Brtko. I've been waiting day in, day out for someone to come and Aryanize me. One Aryanizer or another, Satan or the devil' . . . can you imagine it?"

"Did she give you the keys?"

"The keys? She's going to give me the keys tomorrow. Tomorrow she's going to hand over the till as well, all the ready money and the stock. 'Everything, Mr. Aryanizer, every single thing, you'll get it all tomorrow,' she said, 'so help me God.'"

The hands on the steeple clock pointed to seven and the sound of hammering was already coming from the square, where the carpenters were at work on the third storey of the giant pyramid. Brtko made his way along the wall, bare legs beneath his blue-striped plus fours. The suit, only recently fashionable, with a straw hat, and the slow way he wandered along looking round him as he went, made him look like a foreign tourist who had got up early to see the busy morning in a strange town.

He stopped short when he came to Rosalie Lautman's shop. He did not know what to make of what he saw there. The shutters were closed.

As alone in her deafness as if she were in some kingdom far from this world, Rosalie Lautman was sitting at breakfast in a state of great contentment. She had passed a good night, it was Saturday morning, and once the Sabbath has come all haste must be put aside. It is not for man to desecrate the day of rest ordained for him by heaven. The kitchen had never seemed so flooded with sunshine, and the hand-embroidered cloth on the wall looked more festive than usual. The chimney sweep and his smiling girl, with the words "You love me and I love you" were still clearly visible. There was a lot that could be done to make the place more comfortable; the broad dresser could be taken apart and the narrowest of its cupboards pushed nearer to the pantry, and the washbasin and jug on the washstand could be covered with something, and how many times had she promised herself to stand the cacti in their pots nearer the light from the window?

More out of habit than out of piety, she left the three-branched candlestick on the white tablecloth. The flame of the Sabbath candles must never be snuffed; they will burn out of their own accord, leaving wax trickling down the stem and hardening in a narrow, twisting rope broken here and there by the sighs a lonely soul can scarcely help.

Rosalie Lautman in her bedroom slippers with their cotton pompons, in a white nightcap and—who was there to mind?—in her long nightgown, was finishing off her breakfast. She did not hear the knock at the door, but she saw the door open a crack and Brtko's close-cropped head peep in. Throwing her worn flowered dressing gown over her shoulders, she livened up: "Come along in, now, don't stand on ceremony."

Brtko did not wait to be asked twice. He was so glad there was nothing wrong; that was all. He had hung about in the street waiting for the old woman to open up, roll the shutters up, and let him in. Not until he got tired of waiting did he make up his mind to go round through the back yard. Even that wasn't so easy. He realized that any contact with a Jewess could get him into trouble if any malicious eyes saw him and used their knowledge, since such contact was forbidden by law. The hands of the steeple clock were not standing still, though, and he had to do something.

"Morning," he said cheerfully, once he saw that everything was all right; he sniffed the air in the room and found it stuffy, reminiscent of the night.

"I had a lie in this morning, you know what it's like on the Sabbath. . . Once a week you can take your own time over things. Why should I hurry, anyway? I'm so glad you dropped in. Come and tell me how Lily is."

"We've got to hurry up and open the shop; there's a lot of people in from the country and we could do good business." He gesticulated to get this meaning across, but perhaps he overdid it.

"I know exactly how you feel," she said mildly, "it's happened to me so often when I relied on the alarm. But now, when I'm getting on, guess what. I'm up the moment the birds start singing under my window. Now sit down, do, and make yourself at home."

"As if you'd hear any birds singing," Brtko muttered, and repeated as loudly as he could: "We'll have to go and open up the shop," he was shouting now. "Keys! It's locked! Shutters!"

"The shop? Whatever are you thinking of, on the Sabbath. I've never opened on the Sabbath in my life." Then she added after a pause: "Now don't refuse; I know quite well you haven't had any breakfast." She handed him a slice of Sabbath bread on a plate and poured him some tea. "I've got some fish left from last night, if you feel like a taste," and before he could answer she had got to her feet and trotted off in her down-at-heel slippers, trailing her long nightgown behind her. She disappeared into the pantry.

Brtko did not see the step in front of him and stepped on nothingness. Losing his balance, he flung out his arms to save himself. "What the bloody . . ." he swore and struck a match, for the passage between the kitchen and shop seemed to be getting darker and darker. It smelled like a mouldy cellar. The old woman said she would catch up with him, and for a moment he felt those few steps back in the direction of the shop as a concession on her part; he had to hope that it would not stop there.

"Here I am," the old lady called happily, and her footsteps pattered along the narrow passage. "I'll explain it all to you very carefully, absolutely every little thing." She sounded as delighted as if she were having a party. She handed Brtko a candle to hold and started off.

"Shine the light this way, will you? A bit higher—that's right."

Brtko held his peace like a true assistant.

The old woman started pulling boxes down off the shelves. Flat oblong boxes, some of them big and some of them small, she magicked them down from the shelves and laid them on the counter and began explaining: "Now this is the shelf where we keep buttons. There are all kinds, as you can see: mother-of-pearl, bone, linen, and all sizes and colors as well. Take these pearl buttons, now." Her words came faster as the sales patter took possession of her. "When you come to the price it's not so easy. Now a set of these pearl buttons, that's a dozen, is one crown forty." She turned the cardboard box round and let her glasses slip from her forehead to her nose to make sure she was not making a mistake. "Yes, that's right, one crown forty. Neighbors and regular customers like the Pilcer woman, or Mrs. Hauptmann and Mrs. Golias, though, get them whole-sale price. . . That's to say you get a lot of sales out of them, see? You can go down to one crown twenty, but never sell them at less than a crown. You'd better ask me first." She put the boxes back on the shelf.

"It's no use looking for magic in shopkeeping. Wait a minute; don't be in such a hurry, there's a time for every-thing." She almost scolded him as he spilled one of the boxes in his earnestness. He started picking the buttons up with a guilty look. There was no point wasting words here; should he take a stick and drive her out? Show her by sheer force that she had no business talking shop with him any longer? Buttons were not the same as planks, though, and ribbons were not sawdust. He wouldn't need help from any old woman to wield his plane or his saw; he'd have no need for Eveline or for Marcus; he could manage without anybody else at all.

"Now this is where the laces are kept," the old lady went on, and opened another box. "This is a very tricky thing to sell. It's in fashion one day and out again the next—it can have you bankrupt before you know where you are. Never have I had so much useless trash on my hands as in laces. And just look how the threads catch on your fingernails—it needs very careful handling, indeed. On market days I'll take the laces myself and you'd better stay farther back and deal with the buttons . . . mind you, my boy, it's the easiest thing in the world to measure out lace—once you know how."

Brtko fished his carpenter's rule out of his pocket.

"Oh, dear me, no," she said firmly, "we've got a proper instrument for the purpose." She picked up a yardstick that was lying along the edge of one of the shelves and went on: "My poor dear Heinrich was a stickler for neatness. Everything had to be kept in its proper place. These scissors, now, have been hanging on this very nail for forty years."

She showed him how to measure laces and ribbons, and when in sudden fatigue she fell silent, Brtko felt this would be a good moment and he raised his voice to a shout:

"Mrs. Lautman, shouldn't we open up shop?"

"Now do stop talking nonsense, my boy; I told you plainly enough that we never sell anything on a Saturday."

Back in the room things were a bit more cheerful in the light, although it looked more like a secondhand shop than a bedroom. There was too much furniture for a rather small space, and you could hardly squeeze through between the enormous double bed and the dressing table with its oval mirror.

Rosalie Lautman stood in the doorway watching the carpenter with serious concentration. Here he was in his element; indeed he could forget everything else in the world. He was deep in things he understood, bending down to see how wobbly the legs of the mirror were. "I'll bring my tools along one day next week," he promised, turning to the old lady.

The widow Lautman smiled happily and left him to complete his examination of the bedside table. He was kneeling in front of it as if before an altar. "What this wants is veneer," he shouted, moving his hands as though wielding a brush; he lightly flicked a finger against a carved ornament and found himself holding twisted laurel leaves in his hand.

The old lady noticed nothing. "My poor dear Heinrich was terribly attached to this bed. If he ever had to sleep away from home it upset him terribly. Habit," she sighed sadly, "it's all a matter of habit."

"In a week it'll all be as good as new," Brtko promised.

She did not understand what he had said, but she sensed the kindness in him and was pleased to have so friendly a helper. He was showing an unusual interest in her personal affairs. He flicked the fringed shade on the great, old-fashioned lamp that hung from the ceiling like a pink sunshade and called it a "very fine piece of work"; and they laughed together as the beads swung and tinkled.

An idea struck her, a kind and generous thought. "I'm not rich," she said, "but there's sure to be something of Heinrich's that would do," and she knelt in front of the open wardrobe, pulling out a pile of old clothes. Shirts and underpants, an old suit, stiff collars, odd scraps of material put away for a reason that was now forgotten and almost brand-new patent-leather shoes. She handed him a rolled umbrella, and he picked up the bowler hat from the floor himself, put it on his head, and looked at himself in the mirror.

SIX

The priest in his chasuble turned toward the sacristy, and the servers on each side took a step forward; Eveline Brtko's face took on the look of a triumphant duchess. She lowered her lids and pursed her lips preparatory to accepting honors such as fill a man with delight and waft him to the clouds. She felt in her bones that the great moment was coming now, any minute now. When the sound of the organ pipes had died away, when the smoke of the incense had dissolved in the air, the congregation would start moving out of church in ones and twos and in groups, chattering about the latest fashions, the market, and the latest war news; but first and foremost they would be gossiping about her—and this was why Eveline felt so exhilarated. They would be remembering that it was not so long ago that she and her husband used to sit in the forlorn little side chapel at Mass—and now? She was there among the great ones of the town, close to her brother-in-law, the local commander of the guards, in the same row as the police chief, the district governor and the bank manager. The honors she was now expecting (and there would be more besides) she could have imagined only in her wildest dreams before; they brought with them the prospect of enticing social opportunities she could barely take in.

The waves of sound from the organ finale reached the street and prompted the beggar on the pavement to be ready. He arranged his shabby hat, turned inside out, on the ground between his knees, stuck out his tongue and put a wooden whistle to his cracked lips. He had long straggling hair down to his shoulders, framing an ashen face, and while he shifted to make himself more comfortable as he sat cross-legged, an iron cross gleamed at his throat. He blew a sad tune on his whistle, an onslaught on the ears of the passers-by. If his eyes had not been blinded by shrapnel, from where he sat leaning against the church wall he would have had a view of innumerable legs, processions of legs passing at the level of his head. The piercing sound of his whistle rose and wailed above the festively dressed throng.

Eveline received her neighbors' respectful greetings with satisfaction, convinced that the bows of passers-by were not meant only for her sister. She hung on Rose's arm, smiling out at the world with her full lips; she looked somewhat predatory when she showed her teeth but charming when the happiness she felt confined its effects to bringing out two fascinating dimples. She was convinced that she had hauled herself to this pinnacle of happiness by her own bootstrings. Her light, rather transparent dress showed up her charms to the best advantage, as well as her thighs. She held a white handbag lightly under her left arm while the fingers of the left hand kept going to the brim of her straw hat although there was not the slightest breeze—but the bank manager's wife had been seen to do the same. Eveline was prepared to show generous and heartfelt magnanimity to all who paid her due attention as they passed. The two sisters walked past the little shops round the square, among the crowds moving in both directions. Eveline looked round to make sure the men were following, and there they were at their heels, as is right and proper in the same family. Marcus Kolkocky in his elegant uniform and jackboots was walking along beside the less statuesque and somewhat oddly dressed Anton Brtko. Tono had bared his head and was using his bowler as a fan; be was sweating in his jacket and stiff collar. He did not know whether to greet his acquaintances with a stiffly raised right arm, as his brother-in-law Marcus did, or simply to raise his hat. What luck he had had, to be able to dazzle his wife with such rich booty—what did it matter that the shoes were pinching his feet until he felt quite faint? The only thing that mattered was that they were new: Rosalie Lautman had given him her word of honor that the deceased Heinrich had had them on only once and hadn't even gone out of the room in them, because he was already taken ill by then. He'd bought them to wear to the grave, poor fellow, but she hadn't had the heart to bury them in the dark ground with him. It was contrary to custom. Let the dead be naked, which could also be put the other way round. He had not said anything about that to Eveline, though. The evening before, he had come home with his bag stuffed full with a decent suit, holding an umbrella and a box tied up with string. Even Eveline fell silent at the sight of such trophies when he reached the climax and unpacked an undamaged lady's straw hat and high-heeled shoes.

Now she was waving merrily to him; turning back to her sister she remarked, "Doesn't my Tono cut a fine figure?"

"That's only the beginning, my dear; just you wait until things really get moving."

"D'you really think so?" Eveline was looking at her dim reflection in a shop window, and Rose took the opportunity to adjust her hat, too; at the same moment the two sisters caught sight of Mr. Hrenek, the bank manager, his stomach to the fore and accompanied by his child and an overdressed wife in a fluffed-out cloak.

"Doesn't she look awful?" Rose muttered in an aside; the manager gave them a low bow and the ladies exchanged little smiles.

"She looks like a night watchman's wife," commented Eveline.

"Shshsh!" returned Rose, and they turned the corner by the chemist's, making for the main street. The bells rang in time to their step and they passed through the crowd as if the people were drawn up just to greet them.

Half the town was out. Pinks and yellows predominated over pale daffodil and lime, plump women over slim, fashionable extravagance over sober modesty. There was a liberal sprinkling of gay folk costume worn by the villagers in for the day, and a remarkable variety of uniforms, from those of the soldiers to those of the fire brigade. The two sisters passed triumphantly through the kaleidoscope of color and made for the band.

The fire-brigade band in all its charms was assembling in the shadow of the still unfinished wooden pyramid for its promenade concert. The bearded, fatherly figure of the conductor, smith Balko himself, stood by his music stand leafing through his music, his horn-rimmed spectacles almost at the tip of his nose. He did not have to look round to know that the crowd of curious, impatient and friendly critics was growing. On a fine day the audience is eager to be pleased; the conductor is pressed to perform his utmost, to reach his greatest heights—and not only the conductor; what about the drummer? Plump Uncle Piti, wearing his peaked cap, has the advantage of being town crier as well as drummer in the band. The audience will get the performance it expects even from the gaunt cymbals player, Imrich the hatter; it is his favorite saying that his cymbals are as much a form of fitness training as a musical instrument to him. A good conductor can persuade the poorest of bands to produce divine music, but it is not an easy achievement; here one has to remember that most of the brass section are already of considerable antiquity. Nobody can wonder at the trumpet groaning from decrepitude, at the clarinet wailing with fatigue; the conductor knows all this, but he cannot help jerking about angrily whenever he hears a flat note—it is like getting a finger in the way of the hammer on the anvil. Looking down his nose through his spectacles, he follows the interplay of movement and sound, calling the trombonist to attention and urging the cymbals to come in on time, and exacting absolute obedience from all and sundry. Promenade concerts are intended to elevate the mind, but it should not be forgotten that they have also a highly beneficial effect on the digestive juices. Lively marches drive the promenaders along, inciting a healthy appetite for Sunday dinner. It is said, and there is certainly a grain of truth in this, that when Balko's band really gets going even the monks sport mischievous grins, the old women round the church door in their black bonnets drop their rosaries for joy, and the hardened dragoon sergeants look as innocent as freshly bathed pink babies. By comparison when they start "My darling, that kissing by the chapel I'm missing…" Balko will have the whole of Main Street dancing, forgetful of dignity and proper behavior. That is the right song to play at the right moment; it can just as well be called a marching song of praise, or a merry prayer for a fine summer's day. Balko's baton becomes a magic wand, and happiness knows no bounds—at least, not on the ground. Up there on the high scaffolding of the giant pyramid, deserted today, all is silent. Looking up at the monster towering against the blue sky and the scurrying white clouds makes your head swim. It looks as though the tip of the pyramid, and not the clouds, are on the move. But that is illusion, the sort of thing drink does to you.

The inn on the square offered a wonderful view of the Sunday promenaders—like a box at the theater. The door stood wide open and the sound of loud merriment came from within. Marcus Kolkocky stopped in front of the open door and took Brtko by the arm. "Hadn't we better catch the womenfolk up?" Standing on tiptoe, he shaded his eyes and searched for them in the throng. Then, as they moved forward again, Marcus continued: "Now to come back to what I was saying. You were talking about the minister. Well, he came here and I was giving him a hand up at the celebrations, and then he said to me: 'Kolkocky,' he said, 'you're a fine fellow, but get this into your head: you could have got much further than you have, and you'll get there yet—here's my hand on it!'" Kolkocky flung his hand out in a gesture worthy of a cabinet minister, paying no attention at all to the unhappy expression on Brtko's face. "Then he said to me, 'Now in the first place you've got to put your own house in order.' He knew all about you—what d'you say to that? 'A traitor under your own roof,' he said, 'that's the worst thing of all. He can stick a knife in your back and you'll never know what hit you.' Then the honourable minister said one thing more: 'Then you can bring order to the town as well.' And I said to him, 'You can count on me to bring order, Honourable Sir.'"

"If you take matters in hand, order is sure to follow," Brtko managed to get out.

"'Money's no object. There ought to be a victory pyramid in the square.' And I said: 'Honourable Sir, money's no object, exactly so. A victory pyramid there will be. I'll turn the place upside down to get one.'"

"I've heard you're knocking down the old granaries."

"I'm going to raze the old granaries to the ground. I'm going to blow the old fire station to smithereens, and d'you know what's going to stand there instead? A statue with its . . . with a fountain. I'll flush the enemy out of here."

"You'll need a lot of people to do that."

"Don't think I don't know."

"You're bound to know, Marcus."

"What am I bound to know?"

"You're bound to know all there is to know."

"You're telling me. . . D'you think I haven't got eyes in my head? If you don't take yourself in hand in time, you'll be in it right up to your neck. Get me?"

"I don't follow you. Why me?", whined Brtko . Had someone seen him the previous evening, coming out of Rosalie Lautman's yard with his bag full of stuff? They were just drawing level with the shop now. You never could tell what envy might do. "What are you telling me all this for?"

"That's what for!" Kolkocky snapped, standing with his legs firmly apart and one stern hand pointing at the name above Rosalie Lautman's shop.

Puzzled, Brtko started sucking his thumb, like a child who hasn't quite got the point of his telling off. Kolkocky's solemn warning was punctuated by the martial fanfares of the band:

"I gave you that Jewess's shop, a shop on Main Street. It's got the best situation in town. A gold mine, that's what it is. And what do you go and do?"

"Me?" Brtko cried in dismay.

"Who else? You, of all people. You have to go and act like a white Jew! Just get this straight: a white Jew is worse than just a Jew, because he's not a Jew, he's a Jew lover. You've got one week, d'you understand me, one week to take that Jewish name down and put your own up there. Anton Brtko, Haberdasher. Have I made myself clear?"

SEVEN

Everybody in the town calls the town crier Uncle Piti, or Uncle for short, perhaps because he is so kindhearted and such a talker. The only striking thing about him is his round, tight belly, like a barrel, carried before him as if worthy of admiration, almost as though it were his badge of office, invested with a magic of its own. Everybody knows there is something worth listening to when he starts drumming. "Oyez, oyez, oyez . . ."

Any fool can read out an official proclamation, but to make a simple duty into a performance enjoyed by worthy citizens no less than by the market women, by old men and children, even by the dogs and horses and pigeons—that is more like an art; that is really worth dropping whatever you are doing and going to listen. A duty is something that can be dashed off any old way, but for Uncle (and this is common knowledge) drumming is a ceremony, a festive occasion for an amateur player who has taken the trouble to learn his part by heart and fill it out with the stuff of his own imagination.

That was why the people left the market and crowded round when he appeared. Wherever they happened to be, at the gingerbread stall, the cobbler's, the potter's, they all hurried away from the canvas booths and down Main Street to the wooden pyramid. If you think drumming is just beating little sticks against taut ass's skin, you are wrong. The sound of the drumsticks may recall the whisper of a breeze, the rustle of leaves, drops of rain pattering on a window, the hissing of flames or the crackling of dry branches—and it may be a call to arms. It may be gentle or aggressive, but one thing it must be able to do—and this is the drummer's law—drown whatever other sound may be in the air. It is no easy thing to drown the noise of market day, the sounds of trumpets blaring, rattles rattling, horses neighing, geese squawking, boys shouting and women chattering—the hundred-odd sounds that come together and form the pande-monium of market day. And then, to read an announcement and to read it dramatically are two very different things. Presenting something to someone means understanding not just the announcement but also the public. There is no official document in the world so sacred that it cannot be enlivened with a little fun, and that is why people enjoy listening to Uncle Piti. He is the only man who knows how to put even the most solemn declarations across, drawing out the vowels like spaghetti and bringing his singsong cadences to a sharp finish with the snap of a broken chain. He has mastered the art of evoking respectful attention and of diluting this respect, so that an official appearance can even provide an occasion for a good laugh.

There were enough people gathered round, and the town crier in his uniform cap tucked his drumsticks into the brass rings provided for the purpose on the strap across his chest, solemnly pulled a sheet of paper from the cuff of his uniform jacket, cleared his throat, and began:

"This is to bring to the notice of the public the duty of all dog owners—Alsatians, sheep dogs, Saint Bernards, pug dogs, lap dogs, whippets and other pests—to pay the dog tax within ten days. Dog owners ignoring this order will be pun-ished by the knacker's taking them without notice in a sack with a wire noose round their necks to the knacker's yard beyond the slaughterhouse, where they will be finished off by the provisions of the law at public expense. Signed and sealed, boom goes the law, that's the lot, that's Das Ende, be on guard, boom boom boom."

Even the horses bared their yellow teeth in a laugh, even the pigeons flapped their wings merrily, even the axes ringing on the timber giant sounded livelier as Uncle Piti produced a fast roll to finish off his proclamation, gentle and encouraging like soft rain cooling the heat of the day.

Brtko came up to him and said: "You preach the lesson like the priest. Good morning to you, Uncle Piti."

Uncle gave a dismissive wave of the hand. "Those were the days, lad, but it's all over now. This drum of mine's off to the museum." He raised his head and pointed at a loud-speaker wired overhead. "They're putting radio all over the place to turn people's heads with now. Hey, Brtko, don't be in such a hurry; what about taking me on as a carpenter's apprentice?"

Men and women standing about in twos and threes were discussing the news and moving off; even the tiny toothless woman with an enormous rucksack on her back seemed to quicken her step. Brtko opened the shop door wide for her. "Step inside, step inside, I'll be happy to attend to you. . ."

The festive atmosphere of market day drives away gloom and sadness. The village women could turn the pretty things over to their hearts' content even if they bought not a pennyworth in the end-brooches, buttons, and buckles, with a glitter that pleased the eye and cheered the heart. Not one of them but longed to have her say, impress her own tastes on the others. They haggled over the prices—better talk yourself out of breath than risk being swindled by a slippery shopkeeper.

Rosalie Lautman was as busy as a bee, no thought for her aches and pains at a moment like this, one to be wrought like precious metal, with warmth, delicately and carefully, with decision but with feeling.

"Now I've something extra special for you, dear," she hinted temptingly, and one eyebrow shot up in curiosity as she bent down to feel under the counter for yet another flat box.

Brtko came in from the street like a sergeant victorious in battle, pushing his prisoner before him—the wizened little old woman, thin and tired, hadn't even the strength to resist. She kept her thoughts on her own troubles, with perhaps half an ear for the chatter pouring from her captor: "There'll be plenty of buttons when we're dead and buried . . . come along, Auntie, don't be shy . . . we've got enough buttons to pave the street and still have enough to fit out the whole of your family, grandchildren included. Do you want gold buttons? Officers' buttons? . . . Come this way, please; this is my department at the back, here."

Brtko was supposed to catch what slipped through Rosalie Lautman's net, so that they did not trespass on each other's ground.

"Extra-fine buttons! Shiny buttons! Cheap buttons!" Brtko stood behind the counter calling his wares like a boasting stallholder in the market place. Box after box came down from the shelves. He counted out buttons by the dozen, tapping one against the other: "This isn't bone, if you please, this is metal—the finest steel. Can you hear the sound of it, my dear? It'll last a hundred times as long as you will."

Rosalie was opening the box of headscarves, slowly, as though she were lifting a great weight. There was only one woman intending to buy, but the rest had come to look on, to haggle about the price and fill the shop with their noise. This was the moment of real excitement, when the words flowed easily and convincingly, and when she felt she was speaking to them all and listened to by them all.

"Each one even lovelier than the last, beautiful hand-embroidered scarves they are, really first-class," Rosalie Lautman was praising her wares. "You could traipse from shop to shop all day and you wouldn't find better. Just you go and try, and then come and tell me how you got on. I don't mind waiting, I'm not in a hurry. . ."

"What's she asking for them?" one of the women asked another nearer the counter, and she shouted: "What about the price, Rosalie, how much each?"

"How much? How much?" There were more inquiries.

"Here's a deep yellow one, or a pale lemon," the widow went on, "mauve and blue—you won't find a bigger choice at the stores, not a thread out of place, pretty as a picture. Friend or family, this colour or that, there's only one price: three crowns, not a heller less . . ."

Her last words were drowned in the chatter. In all the flurry Rosalie's spectacles had slipped from her forehead to her nose; as though there was no hint of protest against the price to be heard, she brought the cloth close to her eyes in a professional manner, but it was superfluous to look for flaws in such first-class goods. "Top quality, only the best sold here." Then she added, words intended to carry their own weight. "If you take my advice you'll go and try somewhere else, why don't you? You'll be back in no time. Do you want to have a closer look? . . ." And she spread them out one by one, holding the scarves up to catch the light and enjoying the admiration in the eyes of her customers. The point of the business was not just the sale itself; selling something meant more than just exchanging goods for money. Selling did not mean cheating, it meant gaining by not being cheated oneself. It is a sin to swindle others, but is it not an even greater sin to be swindled without trying to prevent it? "Only the best," Rosalie repeated her argument firmly.

"Satan or the devil, the best or the rest, you'll let me have it for two crowns, won't you, Rosalie?" And a fat market woman with a rucksack on her back yelled shrilly, holding up two fingers to make her offer clear.

"You must be joking!" Rosalie pursed her lips. She did not need to have good hearing to know what was going on. Thrusting one hand toward her assailants, palm outward, with the other she drew the box of scarves toward her.

"You get better at Rubin's for three crowns," one of the women retorted, and the others muttered agreement.

Rosalie only smiled with furrowed brow, as though she had just been told a funny story that ended sadly. She could hear no better than the day before or the day before that, but she had no trouble realizing what they had said. Outraged by the insult offered to her wares—for what else could offering a price like that mean?—she began clearing the boxes away.

Brtko was surrounded by his own troubles.

"Darker ones, please, and they ought to be bigger," one of the customers was saying.

He had had enough of the caprices of his customers, who kept him on his feet fetching all there was to fetch from the shelves and displaying it on the counter. "Bigger ones, bigger ones," he imitated her voice. "What d'you want bigger ones for? Why don't you take these and bury them in the garden—if you water them well enough, they might get big enough for you."

In the end he had to call for Rosalie's help: "Mrs. Lautman, the lady wants bigger and darker buttons than these." He held one up in the air for her to see. "Do we ever have anything like that?"

The bell over the door tinkled and two rosy-cheeked farm women came in dressed in wide, frilled skirts and light-colored scarves; one carried a basket and the other held a goose under one arm. Bursting noisily into the shop, they brought with them the chatter of the market place and its cheerful greetings.

"Good morning, God bless you!"

"God bless your business this morning!"

"The devil's pitchfork tickle your backsides!" an old woman on her way out started shrieking, and the others hopped about on bare feet, lifting their skirts to their bare knees. Even Rosalie had to laugh, for in an attempt to be useful Brtko had decided to sprinkle water on the dusty cellar-like floor. The can he had found looked more like a cracked enema can, and with one finger pressed to the hole in the bottom he directed the flow, drawing figures of eight on the floor. In the general laughter Brtko took over the new customers.

"What can we do for you today, a comb for your beautiful hair or elastic for your garters?"

"No combs and elastic, thank you. We'd like a bit of lace if you've got such a thing about the place."

"Lace, did you say? Trainloads of the stuff—we sell it by the mile," and he pulled his spring rule from his pocket and let it shoot up into the air.

"Just look at the juggler! He's going to measure lace by the inch, would you believe it?" the woman with the goose under her arm called out to Rosalie.

With her face pressed against the glass pane in the door the widow was trying to see the hands on the steeple clock. She was tired after the rush of customers and felt hungry, for it was two in the afternoon.

The watering can stood on a chair by the wall, dripping the time away, while Brtko slowly and thoughtfully let the coins slip through his fingers into a cardboard cashbox on the counter. Then he seemed to pull himself together and started stacking them neatly.

"It's no gold mine, son, you can see that; but it's enough for an old woman like me." He raised his head. "I'm going to fry a cauliflower and boil a few potatoes. Would you like a hard-boiled egg to go with it?" she asked solicitously.

He nodded, still busy counting the day's takings.

"I'll tell you what I feel like having," she went on dreamily, "a soft white roll fresh from the oven, from Brandl the baker's. That'd taste good right now, wouldn't it?" She half closed her eyes and sniffed the air as if she could smell fresh pastry. "Ooooh! . . . ooooh! . . ." She hooted as irresistibly as an owl before midnight.

Brtko separated the coins from the paper money and joined in the old lady's ooh-oohing with comic appreciation: "Ooooh! Ooooh!" looking as though he enjoyed her secret pleasure.

"What do you think!" Eveline had appeared suddenly and unexpectedly, all of a twitter. "What do you think happened to Rose just now? A swindler, a dirty cheat of a woman it was . . . we were in the market and I was helping her to buy a cockerel, and instead of fifty crowns the farmer's wife gave her thirty—the nerve of it, when she'd paid with a hundred-crown note! . . ."

Her manner was so matter-of-fact that Tono Brtko could not help imagining the scene in the market place, the cunning farmer's wife with a cockerel in her arms and Rose shrieking, grabbing at the fowl and haggling over every penny until she ended up with a very expensive bargain.

Eveline's eyes fell on the takings, opened wide, and her voice took on a lighter tone as she went on:

"Isn't it awful, Tono, stealing all that money? Don't you worry, though, she won't get away with it even if Marcus has to turn the whole police force out and the fire brigade as well—every man worth his salt will be after the creature. Just you wait and see!" And as if it was not money, but a bit of dust that had to be swept out of sight before an honored guest set eyes on the table, she put out her hand, held her open handbag at the edge of the counter, and swept the coins and the notes into it with one energetic gesture. "Bye-bye," she twittered, waved a hand from the doorway, and was gone.

"Hey, there, hey, Eveline! . . . And you'll be telling me about honesty! Magpie, that's what you are, a magpie!" He remained dumbfounded, staring out through the street door. Hearing a bark, he threw the door open: "Nugget! Nugget!" Then he hesitated, looking back toward the kitchen. Whatever happened, he did not want it to look as though he was a thief. What if the old lady decided to come back for a bit of change? She might need to hop out for a bit of salt or paprika or something. He locked the shop door behind him.

Once outside, he took the shortest cut he knew, across the square. In front of the pub, he had almost to fight his way through the farmers in their broad-brimmed hats and narrow linen trousers, gossiping on the pavement while their carts, lined up one behind the other to make a wall, made it impossible to get by on the road. He left the noisy building of the pyramid behind him and rushed on, knocking into the passers-by until people turned their heads to watch him. He threw a quick glance into the barbershop but did not slow down until he passed the chemist's. He greeted no one, though people passed him going in both directions. Putting in a sudden spurt as though the tape were in sight, he nearly ran into trouble: a bulldog dashed out of the butcher's yard and growled ferociously, showing its teeth. With quiet patience he stopped to soothe the animal, until it unwillingly gave way and let him pass. He shot into the tobacconist's, looking like a hunted zebra in his striped jacket.

The tobacconist was just serving a huntsman and threw over his shoulder a welcoming "Sit down a minute, I'll be right with you," while carrying on with the job in hand.

Brtko remained standing, fidgeting about and rubbing his hands, trying to make his friend see he was in a hurry.

"Now let me see, I think that's everything," the huntsman muttered into his square beard. "You're sure it's real bone? How long d'you think it'll do service?" and he picked up the pipe from the counter to scrutinise it against the sun.

"If you take my advice, I can tell you this very pipe was made by the best craftsman in the region, sir. This one, and just one other," and he pushed a second pipe over to the customer. "Take it from me you should go for this one. It's not more expensive, but it's better made, better made and nicer to look at. Shall I wrap it up, or would you rather have the other one?"

"Let me see now." The huntsman scratched his chin. I'll stick to the one you said. No, wait a minute, I'll have the other one."

"Take my advice. This is what all the huntsmen and lumberjacks and charcoal men buy . . ."

"Really? Then I won't have that one; I expect you're right."

"Very good, sir." The tobacconist started adding up the bill: "Two, four, six packets of backy, twenty packets of ciggies, a dozen matches and a Bosna pipe, let's see, that's . . ."

Brtko was walking about anxiously while the huntsman kept looking from one pipe to the other, still not sure in his heart of hearts. He put one in his mouth, chewed on it, moved it from one side to the other, spat it out, and tried the other.

"There we are, then," the one-armed tobacconist muttered, licking his pencil. "Eight and six, fourteen and nine, let's see, two and two, eight, fourteen, ah ha! . . . that makes a tidy sum, thirty-eight crowns forty hellers all told. Shall I wrap it up for you, sir?"

"You know, I think I'd rather have the other after all," the huntsman decided, and Brtko groaned, "Gejza!" To no avail.

"The Emperor Franz Joseph himself didn't have a better pipe than the one you've just bought," the tobacconist said; "what more do you want?"

At last the customer made up his mind.

"Thank God for that!" the tobacconist rejoiced as the customer departed and he could lock the door behind him. "If you hadn't come I'd have looked you up myself, Tono, I swear I would. I haven't heard such a good joke the last seven years. It's not even a joke—a riddle, that's what it is; if you get it right this box of cigars is yours. O.K.?"

"Gejza, my dear Gejza, you're the sort of fellow I can trust. . ."

"If I couldn't trust you I wouldn't be telling you this, don't worry. Now listen, Tono: who's got the shiniest jack boots in the town?"

"The shiniest pack boots?"

"Give up?"

"Dear Gejza, can you help me?"

"Of course, it's worth it—the best joke . . ."

Nugget tapped on the door, begging to be let in. He had picked up his master's scent and followed him here. His paws scratched at the glass as he jumped up and down. They let him in.

"What's he doing here?"

"Just imagine this—Eveline came to the shop after me and left him outside in the street. With one swoop she stuffed the day's takings into her bag and hey presto—she was gone."

"Hahaha! That's a good one, Tono, a good one, but my joke's better. Now where was I? Stop growling, Nugget. Oh, yes, I remember. Now your benefactor, your brother-in-law Kolkocky, once he'd stolen all he could and made his pile, decided he ought to give thanks to his lucky star and go and stroke her face. That's a nice idea, isn't it? So on the stroke of midnight—now listen properly, Tono, it's getting good—on the stroke of midnight he went out into the garden and started praying like a pagan with his hand stretched out to the sky. The silly star believed him and his hand miraculously reached right up into the sky and caught hold of the star. And being the rogue he is, his fingers closed round the star and he took all the gold off it and the poor star went out! And since then Marcus Kolkocky has had the shiniest jack boots in town. What d'you say to that?"

"Gejza, can you lend me some money?"

Somebody rattled the doorknob, and Nugget growled at the impatient tinsmith's apprentice with his beret pulled down over his ears. He was so impatient, you'd have thought it wasn't the tobacconist's he needed, but another, more private place. He glared in irritation at the two gossips inside, eagerly talking and gesticulating—obviously an important transaction. Then he saw the tobacconist counting out notes and coins into the carpenter's palm.

The two ran into each other in the doorway. "Is this a pantomime, or what?" the young fellow yelled.

Brtko made all haste back to the shop and cursed as Mrs. Balda crossed his path.

"Well, well, if it isn't Brtko the carpenter. What's happened to my step ladder?"

"Step ladder?"

"What did you think you were supposed to be making me, a mahogany bedroom suite? How much longer do you think I'll have to wait for you to mend a single rung?"

"Can't stop, Mrs. Balda!" He gripped his belly in both hands and made off as fast as he could go.

As soon as he reached the shop door, he saw that all was well. Furtively he put the notes and coins where they belonged in the cardboard box.

EIGHT

Slowly the square filled up with people, and the more experienced soon appreciated the importance of the occasion. Their eyes fixed on the loudspeaker in the leafy chestnut tree. They seemed to be impatiently waiting for a fireman in full-dress uniform, feathers in his hat and all, to step down bearing giant musical instruments from the loudspeaker, even without a ladder.

"A tin box like that and we shan't need a drummer or a band," somebody unkindly remarked to the people round him. "You're wrong there, young man." Uncle Piti was up in arms. "Just you wait until we get a bit of snow. A couple of feet of snow, and somebody'll have to clear it away or all your wires will be frozen up. . ." He looked up at the loudspeaker and fanned his neck with his cap. "What you think, Danny?" He turned to a barefoot boy standing near. "Me? I like the look of the drum and also of that thing up there,' he said, pointing at the pillar. But I think I like the drum best," he added craftily.

The loudspeaker crackled, and inexperienced handling of the microphone sent highly unsuitable words into the air: "Arsehole! When's the thing going to work? Where's that fool got to? Maslicka, Maslicka, hey, you!" The nervous haste accompanied by strange noises, rustlings, and whispered conversations made a curious impression; then an asthmatic voice started yelling loudly enough to make the houses round the square shake like the walls of Jericho.

"Brothers! I can feel your ardor, I can feel your longing to hear our voice, our free voice, the voice of our nation, the voice of our leader, the voice that calls us to battle. Into battle, brothers! Into battle for a united and Christian Europe!"

"Brothers! Together we are living through a historic moment, when what our fathers and our fathers' fathers longed for has become reality." The speaker's voice fell to a funereal note. "Yes, what our fathers longed for. . . I ask you," it went on, "I ask you who has won this victory? What explanation is there but our tireless enthusiasm, for the fact that we have turned out today in numbers worthy of a procession to the Virgin Mary, Mother of God?"

The urge to show off to such a large audience encouraged the boys to practice cycling acrobatics round the edge of the square. The benches were occupied by the old people, and here and there a shopkeeper came out to watch. They seemed to feel it was like the beginning of a carnival, waiting for the floats and the torchlight parade to set off through the town. Three covered carts moved up the road with a policeman on each side loudly hurrying them along—probably Walachian gypsies on the move.

"Yes, brothers," the voice came from the loudspeaker again, "this victory pyramid, in the shade of which you are listening to these speeches, this magnificent monument made of the finest ash, this bold pile soaring to the skies will carry on its tip the watchword of the day, the watchword sacred to all our hearts. In a few moments, brothers, you will witness this historic moment and see our watchword high above the town, and I call on you to hear: Be on watch! Be on watch!" A martial refrain followed.

High above the ground, swinging against the rosy evening sky, were letters carved in wood; as they turned their heads in that direction, they could make out the word "G O D."

"Look at it," said Piti to his young companion, "you can see for yourself—God in chains, stretched on the rack . . . is that a Christian thing to do? Forty years' service and they throw me out onto the street. Isn't it a sin?"

The drummer went into the barbershop.

"I can't stand it out there any longer," he said instead of the usual greeting.

"What's the matter? What's wrong now?" asked the barber.

"You might as well be shut up in jail for all you know of what's going on. Can't you see? Can't you hear? I said so all along, Joe: a Tower of Babel like that thing out there in the square spells trouble. And sure enough, we're in for trouble now. Aren't I right, Mr. Kucharsky?" He turned to the customer in the barber's chair and got a nod of agreement.

Uncle Piti tugged at the barber's white coat to bring him close enough to confide in: "Feel more at home, like, when you haven't got your Aryanizer round the place, eh? Work goes better, doesn't it?" His voice sank to a whisper: "Is it true that he's got . . ." and he shot a knowing glance at his fly.

"Well now." The barber Joseph Katz stroked his head. "He does have something nasty dripping from his ear . . ."

Kucharsky spluttered with laughter.

"I hope I'm not disturbing you, gentlemen?" Uncle Piti asked politely.

"Of course not," Kucharsky assured him, "not in the least. Joe here was just telling me about old Sojka . . ." and he winked at the barber.

Katz flicked his shaving brush this way and that, toying with the silk-smooth lather. He whisked it from Kucharsky's brow to the back of his neck and back on both sides, all over the round head, taking care to avoid the ears. Imrich Kucharsky was sensitive about lather in his ears. "You knew old Sojka, didn't you?" asked the barber.

"Was there anyone knew old Sojka better than I did?" Uncle Piti nodded. "An angel, he was a downright angel."

"Granted that he may have been an angel, from my point of view he had a most unusual head. Covered with little red pimples, tiny little ones, no bigger than this . . ." and he illustrated the interesting little pimples on the palm of one hand. "And these pimples on his head used to shine like fireflies on an August night. . ."

"I don't know anything about his pimples, but he was fond of his food, that I do know. Right up to the last minute he had a wonderful appetite. Lying on his deathbed, he was, and asked for rolled stuffed veal, cut in thin slices." Uncle Piti's mouth opened wide as though he could see the dish in front of him. "That was a man for you. . ."

"I used to do him first with a number three cut, then the number nought, then I'd shave him and massage him and rub his skin up nicely until it was all shiny; he used to like that. By the end of the summer old Sojka's head looked like marble, no, like alabaster, I'm not kidding. I got him ready for the grave, too, may his soul find rest."

"Good afternoon to you all."

"Well, well, if it isn't neighbor Brtko come to join us. Business slack, that you've got time to go visiting? Here, will you take me on as a shareholder, or won't you?" The drummer laughed heartily at his own joke.

"Uncle Piti could go into business on his own, selling jokes."

"And what might your stock be, Brtko?"

"Me? I'm not sure . . ." Brtko scratched the back of his neck. "P'raps I should come back later?"

"Now why should you hurry away, Mr. Brtko?" The barber stepped in. "Just sit down and have a look at the papers. . . Now, to finish what I was saying about my customers that like their heads shaved," he went on , "do you remember old Kohn?" Thumb and forefinger took off a layer of lather and flicked it into the basin. "Now he was a stickler if ever there was one; the minute the lilies of the valley came out in his garden off he trotted to me. Tap, tap, tap—the old gentleman had a stick, remember? I didn't have to see those lilies of the valley, I just knew they were blooming when old Kohn came along to have his head shaved. Poor old fellow, in the end he got something nasty, a nasty nervous tic: he used to jerk his head, like this . . ."

They all watched him imitating Kohn's nasty tic, laughing at his performance. The barber handed his razor to Uncle Piti.

"Just you try it. I'd like to see you shaving someone's head with a razor . . . try it on your throat, jerking your head like that. There you go."

"Brtko's the man for that." Piti passed the razor on.

Brtko took it, laid it across his throat, and they all fell silent until the barber shouted:

"It doesn't take much to make a murderer of a man, these days!"

Uncle Piti started off in a calm voice: "I knew a real case like that. Remember the chimney sweep that lived beyond the old mill? Three sons he had, that's right, and the eldest, John, was a nasty piece of work from a baby. He was a chimney sweep by trade, too, and he fell for his brother's girl. One Sunday, when the other was hurrying off, he said to him: 'Lend me your razor a minute; I'll get the bristles off you in no time. Your girl won't half go mad when she sees you.' Well, he finished him off all right, for all eternity. A razor's like a surgeon's knife, I'm telling you. . ."

Kucharsky's head was shaved to a nicety and Uncle Piti waited for someone to add something to his story of the chimney sweep. One by one they turned their eyes away. "I'd better be moving off, it seems to me, gentlemen."

"Is it as late as all that?" Kucharsky pretended to be surprised.

"No need to lay it on so thick, gentlemen." The drummer got to his feet. "I don't need telling twice. I know everything . . ."

"It's not good these days to know too much," said Kucharsky, making as though to go.

"You're fed up with me, I can see that. Can't wait till my back's turned . . ."

"Uncle Piti, how can you talk like that?"

"Uncle Piti got out of bed the wrong side this morning."

"You're all wrong." The drummer raised his hand. "You might as well know: you needn't be afraid of me. You've nothing, to fear from me. Nothing?" He suddenly changed his tone as though he had realized his advantage and determined to use it. "D'you think I don't know about your goings on? I've got you where I want you." He went on in a calm, almost scornful voice. "I know all about the lot of you. I can inform on you, and you, and you." He pointed at each of them in turn as though it were a counting game. "I can turn you in, the whole lot of you, and make a bit of money on it. What the hell—that wasn't what I wanted. I came in here for you to help me. What a hope! You'll help Brtko, perhaps . . . d'you think you're the only clever ones? Tell you what . . . I won't turn you in, after all. . . As if I could! Good day, gentlemen!" He slammed the door behind him.

"Well, it seems to me you've got us in a nice mess, Brtko," Kucharsky broke the silence.

"Me? I haven't said a thing to anyone. . ."

"Not even to the tobacconist?"

Brtko dropped his eyes. "Who can I trust if not my neighbor?" He sounded near to tears.

"I've paid off your debt to the tobacconist," Kucharsky said coldly. "There's no need to be afraid of Piti, he won't do us any harm. . . I wanted to tell you the Cooperative had agreed to pay you something, but don't think it was easy to get it out of them. Mr. Katz here and Blau the secretary had their work cut out to convince the charitable brothers that it was necessary. They'd better tell you themselves."

Brtko opened his eyes wide. Behind the curtain separating the back of the shop off from the front part a shadowy figure moved to and fro, wearing a hat.

"There's no need for me to introduce myself, I think," said the small man with the long white beard, rubbing his hands as he stepped from behind the curtain.

"Blau the printer," Brtko muttered.

His brush under his arm, the barber went to lock the door.

"I came here today, Mr. Brtko, to tell you in the name of our Mutual Aid Society that we have every desire to comply with your demands, provided they do not tax our poor resources too far . . ."

"Mr. Brtko is a good man," the barber broke in.

"We voted the money to be paid over to you, Mr. Brtko," the secretary went on; "trust us as we trust you, for it was the will of God to make you the instrument of His goodness to the widow Lautman. Do her no harm, I beg of you. . ."

"Now there's no earthly reason why Brtko should want to do her any harm," the barber interrupted him. "Things are just the way I explained to the Cooperative. The widow Rosalie Lautman, our fellow in the faith, has lived a blameless life to the ripe old age of seventy-eight and found such favor in the eyes of the Lord that He has sent her the kindest Aryanizer He could find on this earth. An Aryanizer who will not only help her in the shop but will turn fireman should the place go up in flames, which God forbid. Not even a chicken will scratch for nothing, though, as the saying is, and to this day the good Lord has not been able to discover an Aryanizer who would be content to do the job for the honor of it alone, and that's where the trouble lies, gentlemen. . ."

"It is not fitting to make a joke of it when others find life hard to bear." It was the white-bearded secretary's turn to interrupt.

NINE

Mrs. Rosalie Lautman, who had found such favor in the eyes of the Lord that she had been granted seventy-eight years of blameless life and the precious gift of deafness, thanks to which she preserved unspoiled to the very end the illusion that the world was full of kind, friendly people, felt and in the end also showed her gratitude to the man who helped her. Coming back with the shopping, he began:

"We've got plenty of time to spare today. We'll start with the living-room furniture, and then we can go on to the shelves in the shop. They don't show us at our best, to tell the truth."

She sensed his kindness without needing to hear his words; as he handed her the bag of potatoes he had fetched from the market, she said, "Today I'm going to make something my poor Heinrich was very fond of. Do you like potato dumplings?"

"Potato dumplings—show me the man who doesn't like them!" Brtko grinned.

"The dough mustn't be too thin or too thick. Just right. It's the dripping that's most important, though. I'll fetch that bit of last year's goose fat I've still got in the larder. Wouldn't you like some on a slice of bread right now'?"

The old woman did not feel so lonely any more, while the carpenter had found his refuge at last, a refuge from the people who were trying to talk him into doing things he could not comprehend. He was back at his own craft, although in rather curious surroundings.

First he put the stand under the big dressing mirror right, and then he started taking the bed to pieces, handling the delicate carved ornaments carefully. He took out his tools—the saws, vice, and planes—and put some glue on the stove in an old pot, to warm up.

The old lady smiled contentedly. It was not difficult to imagine her furniture looking as good as new again; nobody would be able to tell it was half a century old. She looked at the fresh veneer on the bedside table with frank admiration, touching it childishly with one finger, reveling in the smell and the shine of its ncwness. "You are handy," she said, and ran her hand over his short-cropped head as he knelt on the floor among the tools of his trade. She went out to look after the shop and toward midday began her preparations for lunch.

In her starched white apron and lace-edged cap she looked neat and fresh when she poked her head into the living room. Her assistant had a grateful audience—Danko Eliaš, Kucharsky's little girl Eržika, and his own Nugget. Rosalie announced, "Lunch in an hour" as she looked through the open door, trotted away again, and was back in a moment with another suggestion: "Why don't you put the phonograph on, children?" She took a duster to the old-fashioned contraption with its big horn, put her head right next to it to listen for a moment and sighed: "This was my poor Heinrich's favourite song".

As she stood by her stove the smell of cooking wafted into the living-room and the music into the kitchen. Lifting the saucepan lid, Rosalie tipped the little lumps of dough into the boiling water; as the dumplings turned and tossed in the bubbling water, they seemed to be keeping time to the lively, cheerful Yiddish song she was humming to herself:

Over the stove, plaits in her hair,
tumba, tumba, tumbala,
She is sewing a new white dress,
tumba, tumba, tumbala.

Who could fail to enjoy such a cheerful tune? Who could fail to feel happy with such a friendly, hopeful song in his ears? The trilling of the pipe was mischievous, tempting feet to start tapping and bodies to sway; even the four-footed listener was affected. Nugget wagged his tail in tantalizing pleasure, putting his head first on one side and then on the other, as though he was listening with each ear in turn. Finally he could not resist getting up on his hind legs, begging and staggering about.

The widow looked as though she would never be able to solve the problem of how many plates to put on the table with its white cloth; then she used her fingers to count it up.

Brtko still had quite a lot to explain to the boy, who had drawn closer to watch him at work. "Meths—that's the most important thing of all. Just a tiny drop and you get all the oil out of the veneer, and then the polish will last. After that comes the shellac."

"Shellac? What's that?"

"Shellac is made of birds' droppings," Brtko lectured him, putting his lighted cigarette down on an empty tin. "They gather it on trees far away in Africa."

The cheerful song was being played again as they sat round the table. Brtko asked for a second helping of soup and went on with his story as he ate it with gusto.

"It isn't the clothes a man wears that matter. . . I was just finishing off a table I'd been mending for the gentleman up at the Big House when a real dandy dashed into the room—silk tie, diamond pin; you could smell the brilliantine on his hair a mile off. A real gentleman, you'd have said, until he opened his mouth . . ." He looked so pleased with life as he chattered that the old lady couldn't help joining in:

"Now my Heinrich enjoyed his bean soup just the same as you, the very same. When the dumplings were just right, not too soft and not too hard, Heinrich always said. 'Rosalie, your dumplings taste like manna.' 'Come, now, Heinrich, they're just the same as they always are; only you've got up a good appetite today, being so busy.' 'No, no.' He wouldn't have it. 'Your beans, now, they taste like almonds today.'

'What an idea! Almonds are bitter, I always thought; is that a compliment?' 'They taste good, Rosalie, they taste good and that's what matters, and that's what I like about your beans . . .'" She was far away in her memories, forgetful of her guests and the food on her plate.

"What happened to that gentleman who tried to catch the white butterfly?" Danko wanted another story.

"First you tell me what your dad says about you."

"Dad? Dad says, 'My seven daughters are seven precious pearls and my only son is an imp of mischief.'" Danko raised a monitory finger and gave an imitation of his father's voice: "'He'll wangle his way out of anything!'"

Brtko laughed delightedly, and even the old lady smiled.

"What are your sisters called? Tell me that."

"I can tell you, I can tell you," Eržika cried out eagerly and began in a singsong voice: "Zipporah, Perla, Rivka, Malkah, Sarah, Leah, Judith, . . ." and the two children went skipping round the table repeating the names as though they made a nursery rhyme. It would have been a wonderful game if Nugget hadn't got too excited and started jumping up and down and, catching his paw on the edge of the stove, brought the plate of dumplings down with a crash.

TEN

In the street Brtko ran into his neighbor. The encounter surprised him, for Balko the smith rarely came out in the evening at all, and at most would sit on the seat in front of his cottage for a while. "Off for a drink for a change?" Brtko asked.

"I dunno. Can't make up my mind," Balko replied, tugging nervously at his moustache. "I . . . I'll blow the lid on them, the lousy bastards; that's what they are." He lowered his voice: "I really don't know what to do next, but something's got to be done. I'll go round and talk to the men in the band first."

"What's happened, anyway?"

"Happened. Happened. Nothing's really happened, as you might say, but there's something in the wind. That . . . that Peter Carny came round a while ago. 'Are you the conductor of the fire-brigade band?' As if he didn't know me, the swine. 'Me?' I said. 'Have you just arrived from gay Paree or what?' A kick in the backside, that's what the bighead needs . . ."

"I know Carny all right: he was born with a swollen head, he was." Brtko had had a really unpleasant encounter with the fool not long before. Who could help Nugget's making the most of an unguarded moment and surrendering to the joys of love when Eliáš's bitch came his way? The carpenter had had no idea what was going on in front of the shop, and, when they came to tell him, he hadn't taken it too seriously, either. Why not let the dogs have a bit of fun? Are they creatures of reason? Brtko gave his opinion, even if everybody did not agree with him, in the crowd round the excited dogs. One black mongrel and one white, they were doing their best to extricate themselves when Peter Carny came up in his Hlinka guards uniform and his jack boots and gave Nugget a blow on the rump with his fist.

"Keep your hands off him, will you? If anybody's going to beat my dog, it's me." Brtko went to the defense of his Nugget, and that was his mistake. His attitude roused the righteous indignation of the self-appointed guardian of public order. "You shameless cur," he yelled, thumping the dog even harder, "you ought to be ashamed of yourself, and with a Jewish bitch, too, right under the victory pyramid." A voice from the throng intervened. "The bitch hasn't belonged to Eliáš in quite some time; the baker had to surrender it." "Bursik brought her," another defended the animals. "That doesn't make any difference, she was a Jewish bitch to begin with." Peter Carny saw nothing to lessen the offence and nobody opposed his view, for the dogs with whimpers of relief had at last freed themselves from their embrace. "Yes, yes, I know Peter Carny only too well," Brtko sympathized with the smith.

"Well, he came in and said, 'Orders from the commander. Eight o'clock sharp on Saturday morning, Mr. Brtko, the band will be drawn up in the square.' What's going on in the square on Saturday morning? That's what I'd like to know. A carnival, or what?"

Brtko smiled, relieved that it had nothing to do with him after all. "Sounds peculiar," he said. "You got me worried, looking as though the world had come to an end."

"All right, all right, you don't know anything yet, so keep your mouth shut. I . . . I'll let you in on it, Aryanizer or no Aryanizer, it's something that'll make you sit up. First you tell me what you've got in that bag of yours, though."

"Nothing to speak of, a bit of shopping, that's all." Brtko tried to hide his leather bag, but it was too late. The smith put out a hand and shook it by one corner until it rattled.

"I thought so! Tin potatoes they sell these days? Now stop telling lies—you've got your tools in there!"

"Any law against it, may I ask? So I've got my tools in there, and so what?"

"I know more than that. I know you went sneaking into your shed last night to steal those tools. Am I right?"

"They're mine, aren't they?"

"What did you want them for in the middle of the night, eh? Going to break in somewhere?" The powerful smith bent his head to put his ear to Brtko's mouth.

Brtko answered loudly as if on purpose to show he had no secrets: "I've been mending the shelves in the shop, if you must know."

"One confidence deserves another." The smith was satisfied. "And since it concerns you and your Jewess, you might as well know: the Jews will all get their call-up papers. They're being sent away to work somewhere. All of them, down to the last one. Don't let on I told you, mind! I'm just passing it on. Don't make me swear to it in court, mind."

"And the swine," the smith went on without noticing the effect his words had had on his neighbor, "think that *my* band," he thumped his chest proudly, "*my* band is going to play for them in the square." He spat eloquently. "Remember what I said." He shook his finger at Brtko. "You haven't heard this from me. . . But you knew it already, didn't you? I thought as much, from the way you didn't have a word to say. It's natural, I s'pose; you've got your spies in high places, haven't you—brother-in-law Kolkocky and company. . . What do they want to drive the Jews out of the town for, can you tell me that? Are they getting in anybody's way? Eh? Do they get in your way, you Christian Aryan? Eh? Good night to you!" He left Brtko standing there on the sidewalk.

Rosalie Lautman had turned her lounge chair to face the window; it was her favorite place to sit, looking quite lost in the depths of the easy chair. She did not mind the sun, although her neighbor was always warning her, "At your age, Mrs. Lautman, you ought not to sit in the sun." "Why not, my dear? The sun won't hurt me, we've come to terms. . . ." Now she added to herself, "The rays of the sun are good for me, warming up the joints."

The steeple clock stood at eleven; the pigeons were circling the steeple and carts rattled along the street in both directions. Brtko caught sight of the postman, but he hurried past and never even looked toward the shop. Perhaps things weren't as complicated as they sometimes seemed. That morning Brtko had told the old lady he would finish mending the furniture next week and had stowed his tools away under the bed. Now he suddenly thought it might be better to take them back home after all. He went into the room on tiptoe and kneeled beside the bed; he could not see the old lady, but he could hear her calm breathing.

"Is that you, my son?"

Brtko shook himself and got to his feet.

"I thought you'd come and talk to me. When are you going to give me all the news about Lily? Fancy her having triplets like that. She is naughty, though, never coming to see me." She leaned on her elbows to peep round, but, seeing no one there, she sank back again.

In a burst of resolution Brtko came out of the kitchen as abruptly as if he wanted to take the armchair by storm. "Mrs. Lautman!" he called at the top of his voice.

"What's the matter? What's the matter?" She looked up, realizing there was something unusual in the air.

"The Jews are all getting their call-up papers. Things are bad, Mrs. Lautman, very bad indeed!"

"Things are never so bad they couldn't be worse, my son. Remember, no woman will ever go on her knees to you." She narrowed her eyes and wagged a finger at him. "You mustn't expect it, not even from your own wife."

"You've said something, there," was all he could say.

Even the pigeons were enjoying the excitement, perched on the cornices and prepared to fly higher or even to fly right away if the need arose. The square was unusually busy as work on the victory pyramid reached its last stages. The carts were standing by, ready to carry away the scaffolding. A wide space had to be cleared, the curious had withdrawn right onto the pavement and the two police officers were intent on their job. Marcus Kolkocky, Peter Carny and Maslicka the newspaperman could be seen in the window of the town hall, as though directing operations from headquarters; they surveyed the site of the decisive battle to come, and it was clear that from here would come the word of command touching off the explosion. The scaffolding was so arranged that one or two touches would bring it down.

"Attention, please!" said a voice from the loudspeakers. "The public is asked to stand as far away from the scaffolding as possible, in the interests of your own safety."

The call was repeated three times; then with a great crash planks fell from the enormous structure. A cloud of dust and smoke rose and shrouded the glory of the brand-new victory obelisk. There was another horrendous crash, and the very ground seemed to shake.

"What's happening out there?" the old lady asked. "Is it thunder?" She had dozed off and did not know what had wakened her. "I was dreaming of Imre. It was pouring with rain all night—did you hear the thunder?"

Brtko was intently watching the street.

"I dreamed he'd gone to the dentist . . . my teeth don't bother me at all now . . . six months ago he forgot his umbrella . . . it's still lying here, I remind him every time he comes but he never remembers to take it. . . Is it Wednesday today or Thursday? . . . How dark it's getting. What time is it?"

Brtko still stood by the door looking out.

"I remember one day," the old lady went on talking to herself, "he had a scarf round his face. I told him the best thing for a mouthwash is camomile tea . . . it was his teeth, poor man, an abscess. . . . It was dark that day, too, like it is now. What time is it?"

"He liked plenty of light round him. Light and a sharp knife, that's what he liked. Just you work it out, Mr. Brtko; forty years I shaved him and cut his hair, forty long years . . . that's enough hair to fill a barn to the roof . . . ten barns . . . a hundred . . ."

Katz the barber was lost in thought, picking up clippers, scissors, bottles of lotion, rattling things about instead of putting them neatly into his cardboard suitcase. In a black hat and a long black overcoat reaching almost to the ground, he looked like some magician, reflected in the shadows of the mirror in his barbershop.

"She kept complaining, all day long," Brtko said, "said she didn't feel quite well and complained about the thunder in the night."

"I no longer understand life at all, Mr. Brtko, but one thing I do know: when the powers that be inflict injustice on honest people, it's all up. Sooner or later everybody will suffer, yes, even the men who thought up the whole business. They'll start swallowing each other up, like fish. The big fish eat the little fish and the little fish even smaller fish. That's the way things are now. . . Imre Kucharsky won't be taking Sabbath fish to the old lady any more. It's the end of the fish. They've got Kucharsky in jail."

Brtko leapt up out of his chair.

"I didn't invent that one," the barber said.

"Are you going, too, Mr. Katz?"

"Don't tell me I'm just being sent for a nice trip, Mr. Brtko. Haven't you seen the patrols they've set up round the town? What about the armed Hlinka guards patrolling the streets?

I suppose you haven't heard they've got machine guns all round the back gardens, as if there was a siege on? All I'm waiting for, Mr. Brtko, is for you to tell me it's my duty to make up a battalion of storm troops with old Mrs. Lautman and attack the guards with our bare hands. Will you join us, Mr. Brtko?"

"I . . . it's time I was going, Mr. Katz . . . I just thought, since you and your secretary said I should come for it . . . the money, I mean . . . once a week. I've got to go now. Goodby, Mr. Katz."

"Goodbye, Mr. Brtko. May the good Lord send you a host of customers all wanting to buy buttons and lace, and rich takings to make up to you for it all. Mind your head!" he shouted abruptly. His case slipped from the chair and his tools crashed to the floor, while at the same moment Brtko came up against the corrugated iron shutter pulled halfway down the door.

Brtko managed to get into Kucharsky's without anyone seeing him.

'All alone?" he barked at Eržika, who just nodded.

He looked round. Everything was in disorder; drawers had been pulled out and thrown on the floor along with papers, bedclothes, and an overturned vase; the carpet was upside down and a cupboard pulled away from the wall. The room was an unhappy sight.

"Mr. Gejza's just gone," said Eržika.

"The tobacconist?" Brtko asked, sitting down on a chair in the middle of the mess.

"He said, 'You come with me, Eržika,' and I said, 'All right, Mr. Gejza, I'll go with you if you like,' and he said, 'Tell you what—wait a bit and I'll be right back.'"

"What for?"

"I don't know. Then Danko came. Danko said, 'We're going to pick blueberries first thing in the morning. Then in the evening... 'Look what I've got,' he said. D'you know what he'd got, Mr. Brtko? An enormous key like St. Peter's key to the gates of heaven. He said, 'It's the key to the jail and we're going to get the old man out.' And Mr. Gejza said, 'They dragged him away from his game of skittles, the swine.'"

"Did they ask about me?"

"There were four of them; it's about an hour since they went away. Look what he did to me, one of them." The little girl thrust out a fist sharply to mimic a hard shove. "Look, Mr. Brtko," and she lifted her skirt to show the bruise above her knee.

"What did they want?"

"I dunno. Perhaps it was because of the pictures."

"Pictures? They took pictures away?"

"Yes, the one with Auntie Lily and the triplets; they liked that one a lot. Did they come to your house, too, Mr. Brtko?"

"Why? Whatever would they want in my place?"

"I dunno. The same as here, wouldn't they?"

The lightning lit up the hilltops, the sky where the plain ended, and the street; it was a flickering light, as if there were a hand switching it on and off again. The rain was pouring down. From the square came the sound of footsteps as a patrol moved away, and closer, behind the church, the sound of hurried feet stumbling through puddles. Brtko turned his coat collar up and hunched his shoulders. His steps betrayed his hesitation: Should he go in that direction at all? Shouldn't he go the other way? A peal of thunder broke overhead, but what followed was not lightning. Brtko had not noticed that the message carved in the timber at the very top of the finished victory pyramid was flickering on and off over the square. They were trying out the new installation in the dark. Brtko made his way along by the wall, and Nugget greeted him with a bark as he turned into his own yard. At that moment the lights went on and then off again, and for a second the words shone down Main Street:

"God in heaven!" Eveline clasped her hands in dismay and ran toward him. "What a sight you are! You'll catch your death of cold. Look what I've got for supper!" and she pointed to the festively laid table as she ran out to fetch him dry clothes and his best suit. "Hurry up, we mustn't keep them waiting."

Her heart began to sink as she saw his dejection. He sat down to his soup. "Is it all right? Want more salt?"

He nibbled a piece of bread and nodded.

"I can't say how I'm looking forward to tonight," she went on.

"What are you all dressed up for?" he asked absent-mindedly.

That brought her up short. The unexpected question was a hint that the promised visit to Marcus and her sister, where great company was expected, might not come off after all. Still, it wouldn't do to give in too soon. "Have you forgotten we're going out tonight, Tono darling? We can buy a bottle of wine or two on the way, and something to go with it... I've done the washing up and tidied the place a bit. I've pressed your best suit, too; it looks nice now, doesn't it?"

"What the hell are you talking about?"

"You haven't lost your memory, have you?" She was getting irritated. "You said you were going to bring the takings home tonight and it was going to be plenty... What are you looking at me like that for?"

"Leave me alone, can't you?"

"Tono, *dear*." She determined to try once more, and put her arms round his neck. "What's made you so grumpy? Let's have fun; come on, now. I was looking forward to tonight so much... Is there anything wrong with the soup?"

"I'm not hungry!" He pushed the soup and his wife away.

Eveline stamped her foot.

"Hand over the money! D'you hear me? I want that money!"

"What money?"

"The takings. Have you forgotten? You said you'd be bringing the lot home tonight. The Jewess was going to tell you where she'd hidden her treasure. All her jewelry. Precious stones. What have you done with it? Where's the money, d'you hear me? Money! Money!" She was banging the table with her fist by now. "Haven't you got it? All right, I'll do things my own way!"

He watched her fury building up while he felt her powerlessness. He pretended calm to enrage her even more. "You won't go anywhere. I know you: you won't stir from here. You're always threatening, but you've never gone yet."

"I'll show you . . . I'll show you . . ." He had not expected the effect of his words to be so violent. "You can have your ring—there are better to be had elsewhere. Here you are; perhaps you'll believe me now!" She was so furious she pulled off her earrings as well. "Go on, swallow the lot! Your wonderful gifts! Now d'you believe me?" She was stamping her foot again.

"Stop that!"

"I'll stop when I feel like it. I'm not stopping today. Where's her gold? Diamonds? What have you done with it? Where's your Jewess hidden it? Go on, tell me!"

"Shut your mouth!"

"They're all going to be transported tomorrow, anyway."

"Shut up!" He was shaking her now.

"He's going to kill me, folks! . . . Hahahaha!" The sound of the violin next door cut across her hysterical laughter.

"Get out!" He pushed her roughly away.

She stumbled forward and then leaped back again. "Here I am! Go on, kill me!"

He seized her and shook her wildly.

"Can you hear him, neighbors? My dear husband's gone mad. He's left the Jewess all her gold and now he's going to kill me. He doesn't believe they'll all be dragged off tomorrow." She was shrieking angrily in his face.

He threw her down on the bed and lashed out at her.

"Hit me, go on! Go on, harder! Beat me!"

She suddenly realized he had lost control of himself. She told hold of his hand, kissed it and burst into tears.

He pushed her away. There were two shrill chords on the violin, and Uncle Piti appeared in the doorway, peeping in fearfully as though he expected to see a dead body. He was in a long shirt over his trousers, with a belt round his waist and his violin under his arm.

"I thought she'd be . . . a goner!" He drew his bow across his throat eloquently before pointing at the woman lying sobbing on the floor.

If there was anyone who had doubts about Uncle Piti as a man of honour, he only had to see him in the inn on Main Street where the wine poured down throats to the accompaniment of cheerful gypsy music in the comfortable twilight, to feel his suspicions melting away.

Whatever I'm thinking
We can drown in the drinking

At any hour of the night, you could find the right atmosphere and the right company. If you didn't feel like company, you could sit alone. Brtko and Uncle Piti went and sat by the wall; they were regular customers in the inn which some said doubled as a house of ill repute. It may have been the two pretty barmaids that did it (never more than two), selected according to the innkeeper's own tastes. Mr. Fedorko was equally clever in the matter of supplies; though times were hard, and indeed the supply situation was unimaginably difficult, there being a war on, he had the most wonderful selection of strong drinks, not to mention the sweet liqueurs. A no less important consideration was the fact that he could offer cigarettes and tobacco in abundance, and even foreign brands; and then there was the meat and eggs and butter—whatever you might care to ask for—of course, shshshsh, only for friends or the friends of friends. But since everybody here was a friend of somebody else, there was plenty for all as long as they could pay for it, and no distinctions were made. This nice little spot had been known as Eden in the old days, long before plenty could be found here in the midst of shortages; Fedorko had kept the name, except for the trifling detail that someone had translated it into German as *Paradies*.

Neither Brtko nor Uncle Piti felt quite as much at home in Paradies as they had in Eden; even the innkeeper had changed a little, though not so much as to show them the door when they ordered no more than a liter of the local stuff to start with. They were thirsty, and Uncle Piti ordered a second one straight away, to be on the safe side, as he said. When he had relieved his mind of nearly everything that was worrying him, he drew his chair closer and spread his hands on the table top.

"You still don't believe me, do you? I'll put it this way: she's a human being, isn't she?"

"Word of honor?"

"Trust your old pal, trust an old soldier—you can't trust the riffraff over there!" They raised glasses and clinked.

"How much longer are you going to wait?" Uncle Piti wiped his moustache as he spoke; it was just a week old. Then he lowered his voice: "Get along and see to it; I'll hold the fort here."

"I dunno, Uncle Piti, I can't be sure . . ."

"What don't you know? What can't you be sure of? You think it was me turned Kucharsky in? I've told you it wasn't.

You said someone must have told on him if they lifted him, didn't you? And what did I say? It may have been the devil himself, but it wasn't me. Can't you understand a man's words any more?"

"I understand all right, but somebody must have ratted on him. They turned him in, they'll turn you in, they'll turn me in."

"So you're just going to stay shit scared, are you?"

"All . . . right . . . I'll go." Brtko got to his feet uncertainly. The inn was full of drunken song.

Whatever I'm thinking
We can drown in the drinking
Of Slivovice and Terkelica

"Well, well, Uncle Piti, what's on your mind?" A young man in Hlinka guard uniform came over from the next table to sit by him.

"What do you want me to say? It's merry enough in Paradise tonight, but it'll never be the same as it was in Eden and that's a fact."

"Haven't you got anything else to tell me, Uncle Piti?" The young man sounded coaxing.

"Nothing for you. You know what people say: better bite your tongue out in front of Peter Carny, but never say a word."

"So that's what they say. I wonder who?"

"I wouldn't know. My memory's not what it was, son, but there's no law against that, is there now? I'm getting on in years, you know. . ."

"And you wouldn't even know where your pal's gone to?"

"He's gone to spend a penny, if I may use the expression, or to take a breath of fresh air. . . It's got a bit too much for him." Uncle Piti poured a glass. "Have a drink with me, Carny?"

Brtko was out of breath by the time he reached the little basement shop on Main Street. Pressed against the shutter, he merged with the darkness, and it would have taken a very sharp eye to detect the huddled figure against that dark background.

The half-moon, fresh from its shower, did its best to hurry across the sky from cloud to cloud, but in vain. The dark mass broke open, and Brtko felt that the light was shining right down on him as he felt for the keyhole. He tried to send the shutter up quietly, but it stuck. "The devil take it," he muttered as the thing creaked loudly. Seizing the corrugated iron in both hands, he sent it flying up with one great heave, and the clatter roused all the dogs in the neighborhood.

"Better wait a minute," he growled to himself, and looked round cautiously. "They'll catch me at it and brand me a white Jew," he muttered drunkenly, but nobody appeared, no lights went on in the houses round about, the dogs quietened down, and only the breeze blew softly, cooling his feverish head and face. There was a bottle sticking out of one of his pockets.

At last the bell stopped ringing and the night sank back into itself like the surface of a lake after a stone has rippled the water.

Brtko felt safe to go in. "Who's there?" he babbled as a lighter shadow against the darkness assumed the shape of the old lady, bent and motionless behind the counter.

"Who's that?" he called out in sudden fear.

There was no answer; his question hung in the air and fell with the tinkle of the bell to lie on the creaking floor. His fingers groped toward the mysterious object, and, with a rustling sound, a sheet of paper fluttered from one of the shelves to the floor.

He opened the kitchen door and struck a match; the flickering light revealed Rosalie's bedroom beyond, like some forgotten dream. With another match he lit the three-branched candlestick. As the shadows flickered this way and that, the furniture seemed to be struggling out of immobility. He crept toward the bed.

The old woman lay on her back, the bedclothes up to her pointed chin. She was breathing regularly, the breath passing in and out through half-open lips. The shadow flickered over the bedclothes, over the wrinkled face, and passed over the snow-white nightcap tied in a bow under her chin.

Alone in the kitchen again, Brtko felt in his pocket. Slugs of wine trickled down his throat, making him even more undecided than before. He heard a movement and creaking sounds from the bedroom. Carrying the candle to his mouth, he blew it out. It was dark. There was a step, then another; the floor creaked and the door groaned on its hinges.

In between the shelves in the shop he took another swig. His face pressed to the glass door, he watched the blacked-out square. The outline of the monstrous pyramid was visible against the night sky. The night was quiet now, and as Brtko stepped away from the door, he felt he was looking into the oval mirror in Rosalie's bedroom and the wind seemed to carry the sound of voices to him from far, far off.

The noise of rasping saws and battering axes grew louder and louder, and then he thought he heard Danko and Eržika, and many children's voices, like a choir of angels. The darkness was fading from the oval mirror and the brightness growing with every moment.

A shattering gleam rent the air, and, in the flickering mirror, lit as though by sunshine, Rosalie Lautman moved as nonchalantly as if she had lived through this moment a hundred times before. She was dressed in her best with a snow-white bonnet on her head and glass beads at her throat; in the bright light she looked youthful. Her long, wide sleeves with lovely old lace at the cuffs were no less becoming than the slightly old-fashioned and almost ankle-length skirt and the white silk blouse. One hand held a sunshade and the other a fan.

Rosalie stepped right out of the mirror into the square, calling Brtko with a coquettish wave of her hand to follow her out through the door. From a distance she surveyed him through her *lorgnette spectacles* with a smile; she seemed satisfied with his elegance. He had put on poor Heinrich's bowler for the occasion, his patent-leather shoes and stiff collar, and carried a rolled umbrella in his hand. There was a rose in his buttonhole. It would not be like Rosalie to find fault with nothing: "You might have run a duster over your shoes," she greeted him reproachfully.

"I feel as though I'm dreaming, don't you?" Brtko kissed the hand she held out to him. Arm in arm they promenaded along Main Street, and there was not a sign of the wooden pyramid there.

"I'm not going to bother cooking dinner today. What would you say to bean soup at Grinspan's?" asked Rosalie.

"Why talk about soup when you know I've got so much on my mind?"

"Everyone has his troubles," replied Rosalie. "Everyone knows what he has lived through, but nobody can guess what lies in wait for him."

"I was afraid of that monstrous pyramid in the square; I was scared of Marcus. I didn't trust my brother-in-law," was Brtko's reply.

"Once people stop being scared of each other they'll trust each other more," she answered, and, raising a finger, said, "Can you hear the bells?"

"Are you sure of that, Rosalie?"

"Oh dear, you and your everlasting doubts," she complained.

Brtko stared into the quivering flame of the candle in front of him. Where was he?

Barefoot, in her nightcap with her nightgown to the floor, the old lady was standing in front of him by the counter.

"Has she driven you out?" she asked with sympathy in her dry, old voice. "Never mind, never mind," she soothed him, "it'll come right again in time." She handed him a blanket and tripped away again.

"Mrs. Lautman!" he shouted so loud that she stopped in her tracks and turned round. He ran over to her and explained in his urgent drunken voice: "Look here, Mrs. Lautman, you know Uncle Piti, don't you? He could hide you in his attic or in his cellar. He didn't give Kucharsky away, and he wants to . . . he wants to prove, he wants to give a sort of guarantee that he didn't do it. That's why he's going to hide you . . . so you won't be pssss . . ." His voice and his hands made an imitation of a train getting up steam.

"She'll have her comeuppance, believe me, she'll regret it," she said with a display of emotion. "Never mind, you'll make it up tonight or tomorrow night. . . . Mark my words: bed is the best consoler." She trotted away, holding her candle high.

There was a sharp knock at the glass door, then the bell tinkled wildly as though giving the alarm.

Brtko put both hands to his eyes to protect himself from the glare of the flashlight and the aggressive voice:

"So this is where our little bird's flown to? And you thought I didn't know?"

"Who's that?" Brtko was blinded by the light.

"Don't you recognize me, Brtko, pal? Take a good look!" Carny turned the beam of his flashlight on his own face.

Whatever I'm thinking
We can drown in the drinking
Of Slivovice and Terkelica

"You see what sort of a chap you are, drummer." Carny pretended to be joking as the three sat together again in Paradies. "And saying we Hlinka guards are thieves—that isn't kind of you, Piti, it really isn't. Come on, barman, another brandy all round," he cried, and turned to Brtko. "You're a fine fellow, Tono; you know why you're a fine fellow, Tono?" and he gave Brtko a familiar nudge in the chest.

"Not everybody can be a fine fellow." Brtko sounded apologetic.

"You aren't a fine fellow; you're the finest that ever was— you're like the tiniest . . . the battered penny that brings good luck. . . Tell you what . . . it's because I've got you," he leaned over the table and opened his palm, "I've got you where I want you, Tono."

"Let me see!" Uncle Piti yelled as though this were a good joke and leaned his belly against the table.

"Come on and look." Carny pulled his chair closer to the table. "Both of you, come and have a good close look. Now the two of you filthy swine, fine buddies you are, you're going to watch while I count to three, and before I reach three Brtko will put nicely out on the table all the stuff he's got off that Jewess of his. You thought you were going to divide the spoils, didn't you?" He was yelling now. "Watch," and he started to pull the watch chain out of his pocket. "One!"

"You're talking nonsense, Carny, you must be joking . . ."

"Two!" the young man in uniform yelled.

"You know as well as I do that the Lautman woman's as poor as a church mouse. Or . . . do you have other ideas? Let's go back together and look, if you like. I'll show you all you can hope to find there . . . a whole lot of nothing. . . Don't play the fool, Carny, it's not the sort of thing to joke about. . . ."

"Three!" Peter Carny thumped the table.

"Wait a minute, Carny, don't be in such a hurry. . . I'll . . . I'll tell you what . . ." Brtko scratched his head. "I'll say you chose a lucky star to be born under, and that's a fact. You . . . you must have got . . . you must have got a pact with the devil to know all you know." He dug into his pocket, thumped the table in his turn, and opened his palm to let the rings roll off.

"Rings!" the blonde barmaid gasped.

"Earrings!" squealed the other one.

The people round the table stared dully, not clear what it was all about and not even caring. "Is that all?" Carny asked.

"Frisk me if you like," said Brtko, putting his hands in the air. He laughed and added with an unnatural grimace: "I got what I could off the old Yid."

The drummer's eyes nearly fell out of his head. "Filthy swine!" he yelled, and spat in Brtko's face. It was all Carny could do to protect Brtko from his furious neighbor's attacks.

The sleepless night ended in a heavy, noisy morning, but Brtko could not pull himself together. He kept on drinking, and the alcohol dripped from the bottle tilted to his pursed lips, ran down his chin, and streamed over his chest under the open shirt. That's enough, he said to himself, banging the bottle down on the counter and wiping his mouth with his hand. Tousled and untidy, he looked like a wild creature running about the little shop, like a caged animal driven wild by malicious sounds designed to provoke it.

Not even drink could drown the noise coming from the square, the shrieks and cries and the repeated announcement from the loudspeakers: "Do not be deceived by hostile propaganda. You are not being taken far away. You will do work for the harvest. In work camps. You will be well looked after. . ."

You just had to hear the words in order to understand what was going on.

Then there was another penetrating whistle, and the loudspeakers repeated the order: "Come to the table to register one by one! Note carefully: luggage must not weigh more than thirty kilograms per head. Hallo, hallo, come to the table to register, one by one!"

Uproar. Hubbub. A martial song performed by the band. The registration tables were only a few feet away from the little shop, in the shade of the chestnut trees. From early morning the square had taken on the appearance of an open-air camp, peopled unwillingly by children and grownups with packs on their backs and bags in their hands. The glass door of the shop deadened the sounds coming from without, but it could not keep out the mood behind them.

"Where have you been?"

The door opened abruptly with a wild tinkling of the bell; the noise from the square suddenly rose and then suddenly fell as the one-armed tobacconist almost fell into the shop.

"I've been looking for you everywhere, tapping on your window and banging on your door. I thought you must have gone deaf all of a sudden—no answer, neither you nor your wife. What in heaven's name, I thought, surely they haven't jailed Brtko as well."

The carpenter had not got his voice back yet. The last alternative the tobacconist mentioned with such matter-of-factness, as if a ghastly thing like that could happen to anyone, that it brought a crooked smile to Brtko's face, and he said:

"Just put me in jail . . . go on, put me in jail."

"You're talking nonsense, Brtko . . . I'll swear you don't know anything about . . . and you swear . . . you say you know . . ."

Brtko spat on two fingers and lifted his hand as though taking the oath, wildly; he was staggering a little.

"You're in a fine state, man. How did you manage to get drunk as that, first thing in the morning?"

"I'm . . . an honest carpenter . . . and that's . . . enough for me. . ."

"Nobody's saying you aren't, but listen to me. If I hadn't seen it with my own eyes . . ."

"What? What did you see?" Brtko sounded suddenly sober.

The tobacconist was transformed into an actor, his whole body inspired, every limb, even the one he hadn't got, as he described his experience:

". . . in the skittle alley we were, Tono, at Fedorko's, and all of a sudden . . . we'd got the pins up right and proper and, 'Imre,' I says, 'if I don't win a bottle of rum off you for this,' and we bet a liter each way, 'I swear by my honor as a bowler, may I wear a martyr's crown if I don't . . .'"

"It'd be just the thing for you, wouldn't it."

"Shut up and listen to me. . . We were making a joke of it and drinking to the next round, 'Get that rum ready,' I shouted to the barman. Then I picked up the wood and made to get the king and all with one throw, and I'd got my hand back ready to let go, like this, and somebody caught hold of my sleeve. I turned round and the other fellow says, 'Mr. Kucharsky, in the name of the law . . .' and the wood just rolled out of my hand, like that."

"You're lying!"

"Why should I lie about it?"

"Everybody's lying!"

"Maybe, but I'm not. That's the way they came for him, as though he was any old beggar and not a respectable fellow, two of them in plain clothes there were, and a snotty-nosed youngster in uniform, and they clapped the bracelets on good old Kucharsky. He turned and called out to me as he went out, 'I didn't win that rum, and you didn't either. You'd better let Brtko have it; he'll be needing something to keep his strength up, won't he?'"

The tobacconist stood the bottle of rum on the counter. "You knew all about Kucharsky, didn't you? Have you heard the conductor of the band has been making trouble, too? They took him off as well, but I heard he'd be out before evening . . ."

"They haven't got Balko!"

"They have got Balko and all!"

"You're lying!"

"I'm off, Brtko. See you . . ."

Nugget wagged his tail and took a couple of undecided steps after his friend. Gejza turned in the doorway and caught sight of the old woman coming along the passage to the shop.

"You've still got her here?" His amazement boded ill, although it was obviously unfeigned. "Didn't she get her papers? Oh dear, I don't like the sound of that. . ."

Brtko started to pay attention.

"That brother-in-law of yours has done a nice bit of work, but he's a bad lot. . . I wouldn't be so sure it isn't . . . a trap."

"A trap? What d'you mean, a trap?"

"Maybe he wants to test your loyalty, see? Maybe he's just curious what you're going to do with her."

"What do you mean by that?" A sober and terrible thought started to nag at Brtko.

"Can you tell me why Kolkocky should leave the old Lautman woman out when he sent papers to all the others?'

"I think . . . well . . . you've maybe . . . got a point there," Brtko had to admit from the depths of depression.

"Maybe Kolkocky wants to see whether you're going to push her out there into that crowd." He jerked his thumb toward the square. "What else could it be? You'll do as you think best, of course, but if I were you . . . I wouldn't take a thing like that on myself, that I wouldn't."

The two men looked at the old lady as she sat there, to all appearances unconcerned. Noticing their interest, she asked: "Is there anything the gentleman would like?"

Brtko took a few thirsty gulps from the bottle and handed it to the tobacconist.

"Not now," Gejza said. "There's another possibility, though." The tobacconist sounded as though he had found a solution, and Brtko perked up a little.

"Maybe it's special treatment because it's you. Or maybe they haven't even got her on their list, as though she wasn't alive."

"She's alive, isn't she?"

"I'm off, Brtko. You're in no proper state, so early in the morning, too. So long, Tono, so long."

Nugget stretched his head out toward the departing tobacconist.

"We can't satisfy all the customers, don't let it upset you," the old lady said. "Is it true that Lily's triplets all got whooping cough?"

Brtko was not listening to her. "What did you say?" He seemed to be drawing a deep breath before going onto the attack. Head bent, he rushed toward the door. "Are you trying to provoke an honest carpenter? Are you trying to get Brtko into trouble? Just you try to come near, you swine, just you dare!" he shouted.

"It's no good running after him," the old lady consoled him. "He'll have got to Rubin's by now." Brtko turned sharply at the door, and the old lady raised her eyes to his. Her troubled glance acted on him like a challenge, but he did not take her words in at all.

He felt full of courage now. He felt emboldened by unshakeable resolve that allowed him at that moment to look imaginary danger in the face. Out of his kindheartedness ennobling virtue came to life. He felt like a knight of old, with a mission to defend the weak and helpless.

With legs astride, he shook his fist toward the fellows outside.

"Just you try coming in here, you bastards. Nobody's going to lay a finger on this Jewish woman here! Do you get me?"

To the old woman he said: "I'm not going to give you up, Mrs. Lautman, don't you worry . . . nothing will happen to you . . . I'll show the swine." He dashed to the door again: "Crooks! Scumbags! Thieving guards! Swindlers! That's what you are! A bunch of scoundrels!" He was shouting himself hoarse and felt tired.

His indignant protest was drowned in a sudden flow of pity. Tears came into his eyes. He began to lament his own fate and that of the old woman and of the whole world. He began counting misfortunes on his fingers: "They've put Kucharsky in jail, Uncle Piti thinks I'm a scoundrel, they're going to make mincemeat of you, Rosalie, and they're going to make Marcus a general on the strength of it all. What are you staring at? Aren't I right? Tell me! Am I right or am I not?"

"What a pity, what a terrible pity to take to the drink like that, all because of a silly woman!" She held her head in her hands.

He was teetering on his feet. Perhaps he had hoped she would talk him out of his fears, but her timid pity seemed to him a cloak for scorn. His indignation turned on her.

"Here I am giving you a helping hand and risking my life, and you don't even hear what I say? D'you think I'm not human, or what, by all your Jewish gods! Don't go turning your head away like that. Listen to me!" he ordered her.

Fear of what Marcus might do in his cruelty and deceitfulness overwhelmed him, and he felt the urgent need to get it off his chest: "You've got to understand! They're getting at me through you. They didn't send you the call-up papers, and they're out to get me. They made me take this shop and now they've got me in a trap, like a rat. That's the way things are, only you can't understand because you're old and daft."

She nodded agreement sorrowfully: "Why, oh why, did you start drinking?"

Her pity moved him, and a flood of reproaches overwhelmed him: "What? You're sorry for me? I'm throwing stones and you answer with tears? Don't start crying, now, Rosalie, I couldn't bear that. Here, here's my sinful head, box my ears for me, smack me around, beat me until you've got it out of your system; it will bring me relief, I'll feel easier in my soul. I wanted to harm you . . . I wanted to Aryanize you . . . come on, take it out on me!"

He was beating his head on the counter as if he'd gone mad; then he tired and fell exhausted into a chair. The old woman came up to him, horrified. "You poor thing," she said, but only Nugget heard her. Brtko was fast asleep. She could at last give him what he needed most—fetching a wet towel, she wrapped it round his head and then went off to the kitchen with the silent dog.

Between nine and ten her neighbor Mrs. Eliaš ran in, at her wits' end. "What's the matter, anything wrong?" asked the old lady.

The unhappy mother gestured with her hands, hurriedly and despairingly, indicating the seven heads of her daughters, like organ pipes, and the last, the youngest of all, the boy. She did it in such a heartfelt manner that Rosalie understood her at once. "Danko?" she croaked. "Has something happened to him?"

"He's got lost somewhere, Mrs. Lautman, lost; we've been looking for him since the morning. It's terrible!" She could not stay a moment longer.

Brtko thought he heard someone calling him; it was a child's voice, or a woman, was he dreaming? "Marcus?" he called out, and dragged his heavy steps to the door, pressing his face to the glass.

The Jews were being marched away from the overturned War Memorial in rows of six; Brtko felt Marcus had something to do with this. His fertile imagination brought the danger home to him. He had to do something while there was still time. When they'd finished writing down all the names, when they'd written them all down and found that Rosalie Lautman was missing, the witch hunt would begin. They'd start looking for her . . . Marcus Kolkocky would point towards the shop. His armed men would rush in—a whole pack of them—and that would be the end. They would drag the old woman out, and he'd be dragged out with her. They'd be made an example of. Look, take note, the shameless pair: the white Jew and the Jewish plutocrat!

Nugget started barking angrily.

"Mrs. Lautman! The world is run this way now . . . there are special laws for Jews." He felt she was listening to him attentively now. "I don't know much about it . . . you'd better look out there, Mrs. Lautman; can you see your people out there in the square? Can you see them getting soft, sweet poppy-seed buns to eat? No, no, they're not buns, they're fish, Mrs. Lautman, stuffed whiting—that's what it is. You like stuffed whiting, nice and soft, don't you?"

The old lady trotted off towards the kitchen.

"Mrs. Lautman, can't you hear me?" Brtko ran after her.

She stopped and raised her head. He crossed himself.

"That's the way things are. It's either you or me. There's nothing else we can do, Mrs. Lautman. I'm sure you'll agree. Can you hear me? You'll have to . . . I can't help it, can I? Goodbye, God go with you . . . go on . . . now . . . Do you understand?" He pointed to the door.

She half opened her mouth in horrified incomprehension. Had her friendly assistant gone mad? She could see from his mouth that he was shouting. "Don't force me; I beg you not to force me to push you out." This desperate appeal

(111)

was equally vain. He began to scream: "D'you think I can't see through you? You're play-acting. You don't say a thing, you old witch, you just pretend to be deaf, and all the time you're as wily as a cat. You're watching me, aren't you? After the war's over you'll be going round telling everybody how cruel I was when I came and Aryanized you, won't you? Don't think I can't see your little game!" He pointed to the door again.

"Get out!"

The old woman started. For the first time, he frightened her.

A loud cry came from the square outside, and Brtko ran to the door. The voice may have come from a single throat, but it spoke for them all, now. Four thousand men and women were trying to resist the violence being done to them, and the noise even penetrated the shop on Main Street and breathed its foul breath on Brtko. The wooden pyramid with the words "A life for God and freedom for the nation" swayed high above the heads of the throng. The people separated; armed units cut the crowd in two.

"Get out!"

The old woman shifted uncomfortably and looked up at him. "They'll say I've been hiding you, and I'll get a bullet in the head." Nugget whined and whimpered. "Get out!" Brtko screamed madly.

Terrified, the old woman took two steps forward helplessly, and then stood as if at attention. Brtko stiffened in surprise.

The crowd moved off in the direction of the railway station, and the armed Hlinka guards formed a chain along the edge of the sidewalk; there would be no breaking through that wall, and he realized it.

He had seen that before, the movement beyond the glass, like ghostly waves piling onward. He'd had to keep telling himself it was all a bad dream. Somebody had said, "They'll call all the Jews together in the square, make speeches, and then send them home again." It had been a lie. They were driving them off somewhere. Brtko was no longer worried about Mrs. Lautman's not having got her papers; he no longer minded her sitting there in the back room. "Forgive me, Mrs. Lautman . . . I couldn't help it."

Brtko didn't even try to keep his eyes on what was going on. The sight of the crowds with their yellow mark, the weary feet, and the children trotting along filled him with horror. He felt as though he was caught up in the maze of silent marchers himself, elbowing his way through the cloud of dust and despair and knowing from the start that there was no escape. He tried to keep it at bay, tried not to see the black figures crowding past the door. "Mr. Katz!" He suddenly recognized the barber. "Mr. Blau!" A woman's sobbing reached him. The old men would keep their dignity even at their own funeral. "They may be going to their death," he whispered.

The force of that unbearable silence and his own immobility under the spell of the word forced him out of his dulled, frozen horror. He felt the need to stir; biting his cracked lips, he stroked Nugget, who was quiet now.

Shade fell across the overturned war memorial; the square grew empty. The man standing there talking seemed to be Marcus; then Brtko recognized him clearly; he was saying something to the officers of the Hlinka guards gathered round the registration table. Perhaps he was telling them that he would go and have a wash in his brother-in-law's shop after this cleanup of the town.

With a single leap Brtko was at the old woman's side. "Hurry up!" he hissed. "Kolkocky's on his way over here, he mustn't see you!" His movements were the convulsive efforts of a drowning man as he dragged the old woman along in desperate haste. "Get a move on, can't you?"

The fear that flared in her eyes terrified him even more and put greater force into his instinctive actions. The old woman could not hear the dog bark and did not know what was happening. She kicked and struggled: "You . . . you've . . . gone . . . mad."

He was dragging her along by force—another step, another three steps, and he had reached the door to the little cubbyhole, opened it roughly, and pushed her inside. The slamming of the door drowned the crack of the skull against the wall. It was a dry rattling sound, an innocent fragment of the moment that was to free him from mortal fear.

An enormous shadow passed indifferently by the shop door. Marcus, his brother-in-law, had not had the slightest intention of coming inside.

Brtko took a step toward the door. He ought just to go out and pull the shutter down or wait a moment for the old woman to come out of hiding. Suppose she appeared in a white shroud to haunt him? He stared in alarm. The vivid image of a terrible apparition came between him and the door. He crept toward the cubbyhole and seized the doorknob.

A chill, musty, moldy breath enveloped him. He would have liked to retreat but could not move. He was held there by the horror in the old woman's eyes, wide open.

He had to explain it to her, he had to answer the entreaty she had not had time to utter.

She was lying twisted on a pile of empty cardboard boxes. Perhaps this, her wealth, had decided her fate, and she could not understand it. Perhaps her hand, lying palm upward, was meant to stress her inability to comprehend. It was so terribly important for him to explain it all to her.

Tono Brtko did not know the answer any more than the dead old woman: the mystery was as much a mystery to him. He wanted to lift his hand but could not. "Mrs. . . . Laut . . . man." The sound that came from his throat was like a shriek. He stuffed his hand into his mouth. . . For God's sake . . . he had never . . . he had never done . . . anyone . . . any harm . . . ever . . . he had never . . . wanted to harm anyone!

He stood in the middle of the shop and gazed with wonder at his own fingers. This was the hand that had made . . . cradles . . . tables on which feasts were spread . . . coffins for old men dead with honor. This hand had killed. . . The glassy echo of a strange voice crushed him. Who was that speaking? He looked round hastily, and a chill went through his head and ears. He knew, now. His eye caught sight of a hook in the ceiling.

The white mongrel with the yellow patch over one eye had been a witness to something he was powerless to prevent. Then, as if a prey to his conscience, or a waking nightmare, he started running wildly round the black, shadowy walls. Round and round. Howling. He howled despairingly, fearfully and sorrowfully, yet so piercingly that he seemed to have understood everything.

A bell rang somewhere near, and it could all have ended like a fairy tale. The children from the yard had been out in the woods; they had not got lost at all but had found their way back to the square, as empty of life as in the enchanted city. The strange silence that followed the bells was broken by Danko's cheerful voice. "Look, it's not even late," and he pointed to the shutter which had not been drawn down in front of the little shop on Main Street. They looked at each other, and then they heard something and perhaps they saw something, too.

Hand in hand they ran, ran for all they were worth, through the yard and through the darkness, through the long, cruel night.

Although he was tired out, it would not have been Uncle Piti if he had not let the children he was hiding hear the end of the story. Standing there in his long shirt, his belt round his middle and his violin under his arm, he finished it off:

"Now they are straight with each other. . . There's nothing in this world the heavenly Judge doesn't sort out. Maybe He has forgiven them all the sins they committed in this world, for you might say they were martyrs, after all. And so it's quite possible they are both up there now, promenading along the Main Street of heaven, and there's no Tower of Babel up there, nor any of the other mad things we've got down here, and there's no need for them to be afraid of Peter or of Paul, unless St. Peter gets cross, and he's a kind man, not a bit like that other Peter round here, that shut your granddad up. I know he'll be out again one day, if not in a week, then in a month. What I'm going to do about you, Danko, I just don't know, and that's a fact. One thing I'm sure of: I'm going to teach you the Pater Noster and the Ave Maria. You'll get along much better with them nowadays than you would with your *Moyde Any* and *Shma Yisroel*. . . . Every age has got its own paternoster and it doesn't hurt anyone to know it. Now it's time you went to sleep. . . I've got so much to do I don't know where to turn first."

"It's time for Slovaks to get rich!" proclaimed Ferdinand Ďurčanský in February 1940.[1] The Slovak Foreign Minister's appeal to greed resonates throughout *The Shop on Main Street*, a truly remarkable book at its time that has remained strikingly relevant throughout more than a half-century of growing knowledge about the Holocaust. Pulitzer-prize winning historian Saul Friedländer once characterized the Holocaust as "an event which tests our traditional conceptual and representational categories, an 'event without limits.'"[2] *The Shop on Main Street* does not seek to represent the "unrepresentable" endpoint of the genocidal antisemitic polices Nazi Germany and its Axis allies implemented during the Second World War. Instead, Ladislav Grosman returns the reader to the period before the deportation of Slovakia's Jews to their deaths in Auschwitz and other killing centers and explores the motivations and dilemmas inherent in what was known throughout Nazi Europe as "Aryanization," the seizure and reallocation of the property and valuables of the continent's Jews.

In his pioneering three-volume history, *The Destruction of the European Jews*, published only a few years before *The Shop on Main Street*, Raul Hilberg identified "expropriation" as a critical early stage in the process that led to the genocide of European Jewry.[3] In recent decades, historians have increasingly taken up Hilberg's insight and delved more deeply into the role that Aryanization played in Nazi policies at home and in conjunction (or sometimes competition) with Germany's allies abroad. Martin Dean noted, "In a variety of ways, the plunder of Jewish property acted as a catalyst for genocide, as individuals, organizations, and governments competed over the spoils."[4] The desire to gain financially greatly expanded the appeal of antisemitic policies. Friedländer argued that "looting of Jewish property …was the most easily understood and most widely adhered-to aspect of the anti-Jewish campaign" across the continent.[5] Once individuals gained Aryanized property, moreover, they had a personal interest in the physical removal of the original owners and the victory of the state that could prevent their return. For Jews, Aryanization prepared the way for their isolation, deportation, and murder. Dean explained, "The steady diminution of their means reduced the opportunities ... to flee, wore down their physical ability to resist, and eliminated their hope of buying material support in hiding."[6]

The Shop on Main Street plays out in an unnamed town in wartime Slovakia, a state that was originally home to approximately 90,000 Jews in a population of 2.65 million. From the beginning the leaders of the newly independent country, which formed from the wreckage of Czechoslovakia in March 1939, aimed to expropriate Jews' property in the name of the Slovak nation. The Catholic People's Party that ran the state as a one-party regime believed that the region's native Jews were a foreign element that had usurped economic control and exploited the rightful residents and owners. One of the regime's leading ideologues argued that the goal of Aryanization was to "create a strong Slovak middle class, which has capital, and which is therefore so important for the life of the nation."[7] In its early months the regime moved to purge Jews from public employment and limit their numbers in the legal, medical and pharmaceutical professions to numbers commensurate with their four percent of the population. From the beginning corruption on a grand scale warped the implementation antisemitic measures in Slovakia.[8] In some cases, the authorities legalized the payment of fees to the state to escape antisemitic sanctions, for example, mandatory service in military labor battalions, but most often bribes lined the pockets of individual officials and local leaders of the Hlinka Guards, the paramilitary force of the ruling party (in which Markus Kolkocky served as the local commander of the town in *The Shop on Main Street*). Above all, higher ranking officials, first and foremost the top officials in charge of the persecution of Jews, enriched themselves from antisemitic measures.

Aryanization of businesses and shops in wartime Slovakia took place in three main phases.[9] First, as during the early years of Nazi rule in Germany, in 1939 Slovak authorities used reviews of trade licenses to pressure Jews to sell their businesses as a step towards their emigration from the country. In many cases, Jews faced unbearable pressure and threats and sold their companies off at fire sale prices to Slovaks who presented themselves as "trustees." In other cases, Jewish owners came to agreements with colleagues or friends to arrange a fictitious sale that left the original management in place. The Slovak Economics Ministry further decreed that any companies with more than 50 employees had to have an Aryan "trustee," who would assume full control of the business once he had learned the ropes and paid off the purchase costs from future profits. In 1939, however, only a few dozen major businesses underwent "voluntary" Aryanization and, in most of those cases, the "trustees" never assumed control and instead contented themselves with a monthly payment from the original Jewish owners.[10] In other words, the arrangement that Imre Kucharsky made for Tono Brtko was hardly novel: It had been standard practice from the beginning of Aryanization in Slovakia.

The failure of so-called voluntary Aryanization spurred Slovak officials towards more forceful measures, which led to the 25 April 1940 "The Act on Jewish Businesses and Jewish Employees," generally known as the First Aryanization Law, which went into effect on 1 June. The law banned Jews from conducting independent business, but also constrained non-Jewish employers. No company could have a workforce that was more than 25 percent Jewish in the first year of the decree's implementation and the number of Jewish employees was to be reduced thereafter by five percent per year until it reached a maximum of ten percent. For manual laborers the limit was set at a mere four percent.[11] Administered by the new Central Economic Office, run by a vehement and corrupt antisemite, Augustin Morávek, the second phase of Aryanization proved an even bigger failure than the first. The state program to prepare would-be Aryanizers to run their new businesses soon acquired the popular moniker, "universities of thieves."[12] Within three months, concerns about misman-agement, bureaucratic struggles over control, and endemic corruption led the government to shut the program down after a mere 50 businesses had changed hands.[13]

In the meantime, the Economics Ministry developed an-other measure, known as the Second Aryanization Law, that aimed to seize Jews' property in a more systematic and efficient manner. The law first required Jews to register their commercial and residential property along with any accompanying debts or mortgages. The Central Economic Office simultaneously banned all unauthorized transfers of so-called Jewish property and froze the bank accounts of Jews (measures that had been enacted by the Germans in the neighboring Protectorate of Bohemia and Moravia a year and a half earlier). The authorities applied Aryanization only to firms deemed attractive enough to find trustees willing to acquire them. Jews who owned shops with negligible value were ordered to pay off their debts and liquidate their inven-tories within 15 days, a deadline that was soon shortened to as few as 8 days. As it turned out, the majority of Jewish business owners more closely resembled Mrs. Lautman than the wealthy capitalists of Eveline Brtko's feverish dreams. In the end, of the estimated 12,500 Jewish-owned businesses registered in Slovakia, more than 80 percent were simply shuttered. The 10,025 shops businesses liquidated in the main phase of Aryanization included 4,036 food and general good stores and an estimated 1,029 shops selling textiles.[14] The mass liquidation of Jews' shops underlines the extraordinary nature of Kolkocky's poisoned gift to his brother-in-law. In all likelihood, a shop like Mrs. Lautman's would not have found an Aryanizer, not even one as hapless as Tono. Nonetheless, the corrupt, haphazard, and contradictory implementation of the Aryanization decrees left open such a wide range of pos-sibilities that practically any possible outcome is imaginable.

The Second Aryanization Law unleashed a free-for-all, where power and connections once again proved to be the most important qualifications for gaining control of the most desirable businesses. In November and December 1940 the Central Economic Office rapidly appointed 800 Aryanizers. Among the individuals best-placed to profit from the law were paramilitary Hlinka Guards like Kolkocky, who parlayed their local power into personal gain. Nepotism was particularly rife, especially among state officials, who legally could not serve as Aryanizers themselves, but could still assign businesses to their relatives, first and foremost, their spouses. The head of the Central Economic Office, Morávek, helped his family and relatives to 41 different companies.[15] To the victor perhaps goes the spoils, but more people imagined themselves to be victors than there were spoils. Soon complaints and accusations ran rampant among the general public and between Aryanizers themselves. Nor were Slovak officials alone in their corruption. SS-Hauptsturmführer Dieter Wisliceny, Adolf Eichmann's man in Slovakia, enriched himself immensely through bribes during the war. He, nonetheless, noted without an iota of self-consciousness: "Every [Slovak] state functionary strove to obtain a prospering shop for himself or for his family and friends."[16]

Aryanizers were technically to serve only as temporary administrators until such time as they delivered a portion of the businesses' profits to the state to pay for the alleged sale. In theory, those payments were to go into the Jewish owners' frozen accounts, which, on the model the Nazis introduced first in Austria, would then be used to finance Jewish emigration. In practice, only a small fraction of Aryanizers delivered a small fraction of the businesses' value. Instead, unsurprisingly, individuals chosen according to political and personal connections, who lacked the knowledge or skills from experience in the Aryanized business, proved to be poor managers who more often than not simply sought to extract as much value as possible in the shortest amount of time. Unlike earlier cases of Aryanization, where former Jewish owners sometimes stayed on to lend a hand and maintain some income, more than a few now engaged in a last forlorn act of resistance: They left with their books or destroyed their business records.[17] Aryanizers' opportunities to invest in their newfound businesses were further limited by the unwillingness of Slovak banks to lend to companies whose leadership and legal status were doubtful.[18]

The impoverishment of Jews caused by dismissal and expropriation justified in turn their deportation from Slovakia altogether. Wisliceny explained succinctly: "Depriving 90,000 inhabitants of Slovakia of income and property will create a Jewish problem, which can be solved only by emigration."[19] Already in May 1941 Morávek discussed with Wisliceny the possibility of sending unemployed Jews to work in Germany. With Nazi Germany's shift towards genocide during the invasion of the Soviet Union, Slovakia further radicalized its antisemitic persecution and in September 1941 issued the so-called Jewish Codex, which at 270 paragraphs was the wartime state's longest piece of legislation. The Codex definitely adopted a "racial" definition of a Jew and laid down an extensive list of antisemitic restrictions and bans, including the requirement that Jews wear a yellow star in public. It also confirmed all acts of Aryanization that had been carried out since autumn 1940. In the wake of the Codex's promulgation, in October 1941 Slovakia's leaders discussed with the top Nazis in Berlin plans to deport their country's Jews to a special reservation in occupied Poland. By the next month Slovakia's radically antisemitic Prime Minister, Vojtěch Tuka, agreed that his country would pay "resettlement costs" for any Jews that Nazi Germany would take off its hands. When Germany demanded that Slovakia provide workers for labor in the Reich, the country's leaders countered with an offer of 20,000 Jews instead. Adolf Eichmann intervened at that point and ordered that the proffered Jewish workers be sent to occupied Poland not Germany.[20]

Although protests came from the Jewish community, from diplomats and the Vatican abroad, and even from political and religious figures at home, on 25 March 1942 the first trainload of young Slovak Jewish women departed, allegedly to work in occupied Poland. Instead, they arrived and underwent selection at Auschwitz for murderous forced labor or immediate death by gassing. After a visit to Bratislava by SS-leader Reinhard Heydrich, the chief of the Reich Main Security Office, the Slovak government approved the deportation of native Jews regardless of whether they were of working age or not. On 11 April the first train with Jews of all ages, including children and the elderly, departed the city of Trnava.[21] Although again voices were raised against the deportations and efforts were made to exempt some groups of Jews, in particular, the intermarried and Christian converts, on 15 May 1942 the Slovak Parliament's act that ostensibly limited the scope of the deportations actually legalized them in its very first words: "Jews can be deported from the territory of the Slovak Republic."[22] Over the next half-year, 57 transport trains left Slovakia for occupied Poland with 57,752 Jews aboard. Nineteen transports arrived at the ramp in Auschwitz-Birkenau; the majority of trains headed to the Lublin ghetto, from where the Slovak Jews were later sent to be gassed at Belzec and Sobibor. The deportation of Slovak Jews came to a temporary halt after October 1942, but began again once the Germans occupied the country in 1944. From October 1944 onwards, German and Slovak forces brutally rounded up and sent another 13,500 Jews to Auschwitz and other concentration camps.[23]

The appointment of Aryanizers throughout Europe not only rewarded German Nazis, local fascists, and their supporters. The pauperization of the Jews severed their ties to majoritarian society and deepened authorities' desire to rid themselves of the social burden. Beyond support for deportation, Aryanizers found themselves bound further to Nazi victory, for defeat could bring the return of owners, demands for restitution, and the possibility of arrest and punishment. Shortly after the Second Aryanization Law was announced, Slovakia's President, the priest Josef Tiso, was quoted in the regime's official newspaper, *Slovák*: "...God help if the Germans lose [the war]. All the Jews would come back. ... This whole war is a social war against Jewish capital. It is fulfilling the malediction called upon them when they demanded of [Pontus] Pilate Christ's death."[24]

In the novel, Markus Kolkocky asserts, "We've never had it so good, and it's only ever going to get better." It is not clear whether the "we" are the Slovak people or the ones with connections or just Kolkocky's own family. Slovakia did experience a boom in the early years of the war when, freed from Czech competition and spurred by Germany's war machine, the economy grew and unemployment disappeared (for everyone but Jews and Roma). In time, however, Aryanization did not bring the promised prosperity for Slovakia or its neighbors. Throughout Europe, Dean explained, "The Aryanization and confiscation programs resulted in much destruction of value, as profiteers interested only in short-term gain replaced careful owners, leading to the loss of valued customers and business expertise."[25] The Slovak State received only a fraction of the value of the businesses redistributed and lost nearly all of the knowledge and skills that the former owners had developed over decades and generations. In the end Aryanization was an act of folly not unlike Kolkocky's pyramid, the "Tower of Babel" that foretold not the liberation of the town from allegedly foreign Jews, but the moral impoverishment and impending demise of the people who celebrated its construction.

Benjamin Frommer

1) Ján Mlynárik, *Dějiny Židů na Slovensku* (Prague: Academia, 2005), p. 131.

2) Saul Friedländer, *Nazi Germany and the Jews: The Years of Persecution, 1933-1939* (New York: Harper Perennial, 1998), p. 3.

3) Raul Hilberg, *The Destruction of the European Jews* (New Haven: Yale University Press, 1961), vol. 1, chap. 5.

4) Martin Dean, *Robbing the Jews: The Confiscation of Jewish Property in the Holocaust, 1933-1945* (New York and Washington: Cambridge University Press and the United States Holocaust Memorial Museum, 2008), p. 379.

5) Saul Friedländer, *Nazi Germany and the Jews: Years of Extermination, 1939-1945* (New York: Harper Perennial, 2007), p. 497.

6) Dean, *Robbing the Jews*, p. 395.

7) Mlynárik, *Dějiny Židů*, p. 131.

8) Ján Hlavinka, "Korupcia v procese arizácie podnikového majetku," *Forum Historiae* 5:2 (2011), p. 134.

9) The regime also expropriated agricultural land owned by Jews in a process that aimed to turn Slovak farmers into "an elite and a backbone" of the nation. See Martina Fiamová, *"Slovenská zem patrí do slovenských rúk": Arizácia pozemkového vlastníctva židovského obyvateľstva na Slovensku v rokoch 1939-1945* (Bratislava: Veda, 2015), p. 131.

10) Ivan Kamenec, *On the Trail of Tragedy: The Holocaust in Slovakia*, trans. by Martin Styan (Bratislava: H&H, 2007), pp. 77-80.

11) Kamenec, *On the Trail of Tragedy*, pp. 87-94.

12) Mlynárik, *Dějiny Židů*, p. 134.

13) Kamenec, *On the Trail of Tragedy*, pp. 94-95.

14) Kamenec, *On the Trail of Tragedy*, p. 138.

15) Kamenec, *On the Trail of Tragedy*, p. 150.

16) Kamenec, *On the Trail of Tragedy*, p. 147.

17) Kamenec, *On the Trail of Tragedy*, p. 143.

18) Kamenec, *On the Trail of Tragedy*, pp. 90-91, 141.

19) Kamenec, *On the Trail of Tragedy*, p. 153.

20) Mlynárik, *Dějiny Židů*, pp. 158-162.

21) Mlynárik, *Dějiny Židů*, p. 193.

22) Kamenec, *On the Trail of Tragedy*, pp. 237-41.

23) Mlynárik, *Dějiny Židů*, p. 198; Kamenec, *On the Trail of Tragedy*, pp. 246 and 337.

24) Mlynárik, *Dějiny Židů*, p. 137.

25) Dean, *Robbing the Jews*, p. 394.

The modern history of Central Europe is notable for its political and cultural discontinuities and often violent changes, as well as its attempts to preserve and (re)invent traditional cultural identities. This series cultivates contemporary translations of influential literary works that have been unavailable to a global readership due to censorship, the effects of the Cold War and the frequent political disruptions in Czech publishing and its international ties. Readers of English, in today's cosmopolitan Prague and anywhere in the physical and electronic world, can now become acquainted with works that capture the Central European historical experience. Works that helped express and form Czech and Central European identity, humour and imagination. Believing that any literary canon can be defined only in dialogue with other cultures, the series publishes classics, often used in Western university courses, as well as (re)discoveries aiming to provide new perspectives in intermedial studies of literature, history and culture. All titles are accompanied by an afterword. Translations are reviewed and circulated in the global scholarly community before publication – this is reflected by our nominations for several literary awards.

Published titles
Zdeněk Jirotka: Saturnin (2003, 2005, 2009, 2013; pb 2016)
Vladislav Vančura: Summer of Caprice (2006; pb 2016)
Karel Poláček: We Were a Handful (2007; pb 2016)
Bohumil Hrabal: Pirouettes on a Postage Stamp (2008)
Karel Michal: Everyday Spooks (2008)
Eduard Bass: The Chattertooth Eleven (2009)
Jaroslav Hašek: Behind the Lines: Bugulma and Other Stories (2012; pb 2016)
Bohumil Hrabal: Rambling On (2014; pb 2016)
Ladislav Fuks: Of Mice and Mooshaber (2014)
Josef Jedlička: Midway Upon the Journey of Our Life (2016)
Jaroslav Durych: God's Rainbow (2016)
Ladislav Fuks: The Cremator (2016)
Bohuslav Reynek: The Well at Morning (2017)
Viktor Dyk: The Pied Piper (2017)
Jiří R. Pick: Society for the Prevention of Cruelty to Animals (2018)
Views from the Inside: Czech Underground Literature and Culture (1948–1989), ed. M. Machovec (2018)

Forthcoming
Jiří Pelán: Bohumil Hrabal: A Full-length Portrait
Bohumil Hrabal: Why I Write? The Early Prose from 1945 to 1952
Ludvík Vaculík: A Czech Dreambook
Jan Čep: Common Rue: Short Stories
Jiří Weil: Lamentation for 77,297 Victims